D0253861

RON'S GONE WRONG

THE OFFICIAL MOVIE NOVELIZATION

PENGUIN YOUNG READERS LICENSES
An Imprint of Penguin Random House LLC, New York

© 2021 20th Century Studios

Published by Penguin Young Readers Licenses,
an imprint of Penguin Random House LLC, New York.
Printed in the USA.

Visit us online at www.penguinrandomhouse.com.

ISBN 9780593094600   10 9 8 7 6 5 4 3 2 1

RON'S GONE WRONG

THE OFFICIAL
MOVIE NOVELIZATION

BY KIEL PHEGLEY

Directed by: Jean-Philippe Vine, Sarah Smith
Written by: Peter Baynham & Sarah Smith
Produced by: Julie Lockhart, Lara Breay

CHAPTER 1
LAUNCH DAY

Everyone could remember where they were the day the B*Bots arrived. It was broadcast across TV stations, live feeds, streaming services, and phone screens to an audience of billions. Bubble, the coolest high-tech company on planet Earth, had done it again. But this time what they were promising was a product smarter than the smartest phone and more social than any social media app. They were promising a new kind of friend for everyone.

Like the rest of the world, Barney Pudowski watched the product launch live. In his living room, the aging Pudowski television, which, thanks to his gran's meddling, kept switching to bizarre game shows, flickered weakly with the news report of the launch. Barney could see himself—messy hair, funny ears, and

1

nervous face — in the reflection. As images streamed past of previous Bubble triumphs, it was almost like he was there. Like Barney could almost really own a piece of Bubble tech. *Almost.*

This was a classic Bubble Corporation announcement. Fans had camped out late the night before at Bubble's headquarters, bouncing with excitement on their street-worn sleeping bags. Behind them, the massive glass exterior of the Bubble Dome loomed large. Set atop a huge dam deep in the mountains, the futuristic dome glimmered like a dream factory, holding the secret of their next life-altering device.

"So, you've been here awhile . . . What are you hoping for?" a TV reporter asked a bleary-eyed fan toward the front of the line.

"I dunno . . . like AR, VR, split view . . . a calendar that projects onto your face! It's Bubble. I just want one!" he crowed.

When the moment finally arrived, the cameras joined the rush of people through the glass doors and into the amazing, high-tech lobby of the Bubble Dome. Just like the company's signature worldwide storefronts, the Bubble Dome was staffed at every polished countertop with Bubble Buddies. This staff led the crowd as they pushed, prodded, and fist-pumped their way around an empty stage at the heart of the dome.

The lights in the dome dimmed, and Barney leaned in toward his TV screen. His breath fogged the surface in anticipation. Any moment now, the most famous tech company in the world would unveil their latest.

Spotlights snapped to life, revealing Marc Wydell, Bubble's genius CEO. His hair and clothes were scruffy, and he shied away from the lights onstage, squinting through eyes that had spent all day staring at algorithms flashing across his screen. But he still smiled to the crowd. Behind Marc, as always, stood Andrew Morris, the wiry chief operating officer. Andrew grinned at the crowd, decked out in his ever-present black T-shirt as his phone, watch, and earpiece shimmered with the latest Bubble wearable tech.

"We did this together, guys!" Marc raised his hands in the air. "This is what it's all been for, right back to the time in the garage where Bubble started."

"My garage, folks . . . my garage . . . ," Andrew

said, laughing and leaning in.

"Of course, yes, my amazing partner, Andrew . . .
thanks for the, um, the garage," Marc said with an
awkward laugh. "But let me ask you all a question: Have
you ever felt completely alone? Standing on the edge
of things, not daring to approach anyone? What if you
could have the perfect friend? Someone who thinks
you're awesome and who could help you find other
friends with ease.

"Well, today we take a huge leap—from Bubble's
phones and tablets and watches—to a whole new
world of connection," Marc Wydell continued, his voice
growing more excited as Barney's heart started to race
like he was in the room, too. "At the heart of Bubble's
latest is the program I've been working on for ten years.
My code. My algorithm for friendship!"

Barney couldn't help but clap his hands excitedly at
home as the crowd at the Bubble Dome went wild. Just
looking at the man, it would be impossible to guess how
famous Marc Wydell was. But the code Marc wrote
had already changed the lives of everyone that touched it.

Using a Bubble tech device was more than a
status symbol. It was a part of life. If you didn't have

a BubblePad, BubblePhone, or BubbleTop personal computer, you basically didn't exist, as Barney knew all too well.

With all eyes on him, Marc pulled up a name in his phone and scanned the crowd. "Do we have an EllieB9 here?"

A little girl a few years younger than Barney, maybe nine, sprinted up to the stage. Her eyes widened with excitement as a Bubble drone lowered a gleaming, egg-shaped package onto the stage. At about three feet tall, this had to be the biggest piece of Bubble technology Barney had ever seen.

"Hi, Ellie. This is for you. The world's very first Bubble Bot," Marc Wydell said.

The girl reached out and touched the package's surface. The pristine white face of the device shivered to life, unfolding and unwrapping itself like a flower until it had reconfigured as a simple but gorgeous translucent pill-shaped body. A glowing heart came to life under Ellie's hand.

"What's happening?" she said as Marc walked behind the device, tapping away at the phone in his hand.

"It's getting to know you!" the CEO explained. "Everything about you. As the B*Bot connects to your Bubble profile, my algorithm shapes its personality to yours." Marc offered a final tap to send Ellie's data profile, and with a blink, a small face on the device came to life.

"Hi, Ellie," said the B*Bot, tilting its eyes warmly. The bot's surface instantaneously recolored itself with the recognizable uniform of a cartoon rabbit.

"Danger-Bunny?" Ellie said with a grin. "That's my favorite show. I like to watch it and pretend I'm an astronaut."

"Me too!" the bot held out a tiny flap of a hand. "Do you wanna play?"

"The B*Bot has an infinite number of downloadable skins, apps, contacts, photos, chats . . . music, too, of course," Marc announced as the bot began to shimmer and change color to a pulsing beat. "There's a three-hundred-and-sixty-degree immersive projection, powered by its constant connection to the Bubble Network! And that network, of course, controls the B*Bot's incredible safety settings to keep your parents happy!"

Ellie gasped as her B*Bot spun and switched its skin a dozen times in a minute. Puppies! Race cars! Monkeys! Any character, app, or concept Ellie had ever awarded a like to on her BubblePhone was fair game as the bot spun around the stage.

"You can be anything in the world?" asked Ellie, completely awed.

"In the *universe*!" her B*Bot replied.

The bot skinned as a rocket. Somewhere on the translucent shell, a hidden projector arrayed a kaleidoscope of light in all directions, and suddenly it was as if Ellie was taking off through the Earth's atmosphere, then standing on Mars.

But best of all was when the B*Bot started connecting her with the other kids in the audience. With a rhythmic pinging sound, Ellie's B*Bot scanned the room for compatible Bubble profiles, finally zeroing in on a pair of kids hopping with excitement at the edge of the crowd.

The B*Bot zoomed in their direction and nudged the kids toward the stage. "This is Pete66 and GraceMay11," it said. "They want to be astronauts, too. Come make friends with Ellie!"

The audience went wild as Marc Wydell shouted from the stage again, his arms thrust in the air. "Your Best Friend Out of the Box!" he cried as the tagline lit up the stage. "Let's do this! LET'S MAKE FRIENDS!"

It was all Barney Pudowski needed to see. It was all he could think about. But it was also the worst moment of his life, because Barney knew that unless something changed in a big way, he'd never get a B*Bot of his own. And that meant he'd never make a friend.

CHAPTER 2
BIRTHDAY NOTIFICATION

It was mere weeks before B*Bots were everywhere. Kids dragged their parents to Bubble Stores in record numbers. Lines stretched around the block as what seemed like every middle schooler in America walked in with a set of data and walked out with a personalized Best Friend Out of the Box.

Well, almost every middle schooler . . .

The fateful fall morning began like most others. Barney pushed his ramshackle scooter through the streets of the sleepy suburb of Nonsuch, trying not to stand out. He'd been invisible to the other kids in his neighborhood for so long that it felt like forever. And at this point, he almost preferred to be unseen, unnoticed.

But the bright yellow safety vest wasn't helping.

"Barney!" called his grandmother, Donka, as he started out the door that morning. "You have safety vest?" She never let him get too far without wrapping him up in the gaudy pullover and her own worries.

"I've got it, Gran!" he said, tugging at the ugly, itchy neon cover.

"And you have lunch? I gave you extra cheese banitsas and chicken feet for your big day! And you have inhaler? Can't have asthma attack on day of birth!"

"I've got it all, Gran! I promise!"

"And you have special party invites?"

Barney pushed one foot off his scooter and rolled down the lane without answering. The dry patch of grass that marked their house at the top of the hill, and the goat, which had eaten the lawn to pieces, receded into the background. Out of sight of the house, he stuffed the safety vest into his backpack and turned toward downtown. Barney felt bad—Donka only wanted what was best for him. She'd done so much for both him and Dad after they lost Mom. But it was hard to stay invisible when she was barreling through the streets in her ancient pickup truck, overflowing with chicken wire and rusted power tools, pumping out

10

Bulgaria's most famous 1970s pop star, Zany Bogomil.

Their ancient truck and old ways made it hard to stay invisible in Nonsuch especially. As that summer turned into the new school year, the town's rows of low houses became littered with futuristic scenes from Barney's wildest dreams. In one direction, a boy swatted a foam sword at a green-skinned Orc B*Bot. Around a corner, girls sped along on a pair of Racer B*Bots. Scuba-diving B*Bots projected an undersea world along the underpass. And was that a Ninja B*Bot sneaking across the street?

It seemed like every day new B*Bots rolled out of the Bubble Store in Nonsuch's town square. Like ants out of a hill, the pill-shaped pals flew. Their skins were ever-shifting to superheroes, sea serpents, princess ponies, and pirate captains.

As he turned the scooter through the square that morning, Barney watched as the latest B*Bot purchase swung out the door, holding the hand of a kid younger than him. Barney pushed himself toward school slowly. As the kid and his bot skipped off happily, the gleaming exterior of the huge dome-shaped store called to Barney. He finally stopped, staring longingly at its doors and —

Crash!

"You got eyes, kid?" shouted a Bubble van delivery driver as Barney looked up from the ground where he'd fallen to his knees. He'd stopped in moving traffic! Thankfully, the van had screeched to a halt just in time to avoid flattening Barney.

"Sorry! I'm so sorry!" Barney stammered and picked up his scooter. As he rolled past quickly, he took one last glance behind him. The driver leaned over a pile of Bubble boxes that had fallen off the tailgate when he had skidded to a stop. One of the big containers had dented badly when it hit the ground.

As he rounded the last block and approached Nonsuch Middle School, Barney tried to shake off the embarrassment of his accident. The arrival of the B*Bots had taken hanging out to the next level everywhere on campus. Goth kids were haunted by vampire-skinned bots in the shadowy edges of the hallway while comic book fans battled from classroom to classroom like they lived in a graphic novel. Barney shuffled past packs of older kids acting out the latest internet meme with their bots, and with each robotic

12

chirp, he felt more and more invisible.

Through the open doorway of a classroom, Ava was giving a presentation to a gaggle of lab-obsessed science kids. "So, you see how the magma from the upper mantle pushes up into the chamber?" She modeled on a real-time volcano demo projected onto the wall. Everyone in Ava's crowd knew that, from her ripped jeans and short hair to her razor-sharp mind, this girl was going to split atoms someday. And Barney privately marveled at how she just didn't seem to care about being popular, how she was above it all.

"Guys, is she coming yet? This is going to be crazy!" rang a familiar voice over Barney's shoulder.

Rich Belcher crouched behind a hallway corner while his ever-present friends Jayden and Alex flanked him and giggled. Like always, Rich was decked out in a fresh-off-the-rack, oversize ski jacket with a matching ball cap and B*Bot. Rich was the self-proclaimed BubbleTube prankmaster, with a channel called Prank You Very Much—watched only by Jayden, Alex, and himself, and every day was a quest for new subscribers.

Barney crossed the hall to get to his locker and hopefully escape the notice of Rich's crew, but instead found himself in the path of the Queen Bee of Nonsuch Middle School: Savannah Meades.

She strode down the hall with the purpose and poise she'd had since kindergarten. Savannah was always a flawless portrait. Her dark flowing hair flipped out at exactly the right angle. Her satin jacket sparkled with the reflection of her B*Bot's disco ball skin. Even her sneakers were pearly white. Of course, she had to look perfect since she was broadcasting to the web almost 24-7.

"Hey, guys! Savannah here," she spoke into her stylish B*Bot's camera with a wink. "So, later I wanna talk to you guys about plastics in the ocean, and this new great blowout!"

"Sixty-three people love that, Sav!" said the bot.

"Gwaaaaaar!" Rich leaped from his hiding spot and into Sav's path, wearing a zombie mask. He rolled on the floor making growling noises and failing to register the lack of reaction on Sav's face as his B*Bot spun around trying to get the perfect reaction angle.

"Lame, Rich," Savannah said, stepping over him. She walked past gracefully as Rich peeled the mask from his face and scowled.

"Top quality footage," said his B*Bot in a loud, encouraging voice.

"Yeah, bro! Only the best!" Jayden offered a forced laugh as he pulled his leader up from the floor.

"Uh, yeah! She totally flinched!" Rich recovered and tossed his blond bangs to get back into his "pranksona." He leaned into the B*Bot's camera to sign off. "Don't forget to like and subscribe!"

Barney opened his locker, relieved, until—

"Weep, trollboy! I am fire!"

As that battle cry pierced his eardrums, a speeding metal shell that could only be a B*Bot rocked Barney's body and sent his head spinning. Just the same as with the van that morning, he crashed to the floor hard, and the contents of his backpack scattered across the hall. Barney's asthma inhaler ricocheted to his left. The cheese banitsa lunch spilled out to his right. But that wasn't worst of all.

Noah Lee lifted Barney off the ground. It was the school's superstar gamer's stat-pumping B*Bot that had knocked Barney down. But just then, it didn't even register that the pair had paused their competition to drag him onto his feet. What mattered to Barney in that moment was what became of the pink envelopes he'd hidden deep in his bag.

And then he saw that they had fallen right at Savannah's feet.

"Barney is having a party," her B*Bot announced.

"Wow, Barney, it's your birthday?" Savannah said with a look equal parts pity and kindness. "And you still didn't get a B*Bot?"

He could barely hear the question. Everyone was looking at him now.

"No!" Barney panicked. "No party. No birthday, really." He swiped the invite out of her hand and stuffed it in among his now loose lunch, praying no one had seen the chicken feet.

"I'll just get out of your shot," Barney said.

"Oh, that's okay, Barney," she replied, awkward and not wanting to offend him. "I actually have a filter that will do that for me." And with that, he disappeared from her B*Bot's screen.

Barney rushed around the first corner he could and pumped his inhaler into his lungs once for good measure. He was exhausted. He was alone. And most days, that wasn't so bad, but it was getting harder and harder to stay invisible in a B*Bot world. He headed into his morning class.

Even recess ended up turning into a nightmare for Barney. He had made a habit out of hiding in a dark corner of the school yard and counting the minutes until the bell rang. But now that the B*Bots had turned the entire school into an augmented reality sandbox, Barney had resorted to sneaking back inside and waiting it out in an empty classroom.

"What's this, all alone on your birthday?" Barney's stomach dropped at the sound of the sickly sweet Miss Thomas. Despite Barney's best efforts, Miss Thomas had taken it upon herself to help him make friends. Barney tried to explain that drawing attention to himself was only making things worse, but Miss Thomas had taken a class, and when people have taken a class, nothing can stop them.

His protests fell on deaf ears as she steered him over to the Friendstop, the schoolyard's designated landing area for the awkward and alone, plonking him down under a sign that read "Need a friend? One will be along soon!"

"Now, when someone comes along, talk to them

about . . . a hobby!" Miss Thomas said in a gentle, rehearsed sort of voice. "Didn't you write me an essay on rock collecting?"

Barney wondered why he had been so stupid as to let slip in an essay that he was into rock collecting, as Miss Thomas hurried around the playground, stage whispering something to Noah, Savannah, and Ava.

It's okay, Barney thought to himself, *these guys are okay. They'll forget about it. As long as she doesn't ask them to —*

"Will you go talk to Barney . . . he loves rocks . . . it's his birthday . . ." Miss Thomas's words to the others sunk into Barney's ears like a bomb blast.

"Wait, what? Rocks?!" Barney's heart sank as Rich's loud, gleeful voice rang out across the packed yard. *"Rocks?!"*

CHAPTER 3
UNBOXING

Barney rolled home after school with a backpack still full of invites and his ears still ringing with Rich's "hilarious" puns that had followed him around all afternoon ("You're a rock star, Barney!" "Who's your favorite movie star? The Rock?!" "Rock on, dude!").

Inside the house, Donka was already boiling lamb stomachs in the kitchen. Even with a grandmother who seemed to have transported the old country with her rather than having left it behind, a full-on formal dinner was a rare thing in the Pudowski house. Barney felt his heart drop as he walked down the corridor and smelled the tangy steam of it, remembering what he had gotten himself into.

"Sorry . . . are we? Are we on the line?" Dad's voice rang out from his cluttered home office. "Yes, hello! Today, Mr. Takahashi, we here at Pudowski Novelty Exports International are very excited to offer you . . . the, uh, Brother Bouncy Car Monk!"

Dad was scrambling to find a potential buyer for any of the crates of discount knickknacks and pop-up figurines that sat stacked all around his desk . . . and in his bedroom . . . and in the family garage. Barney leaned on the door to witness the latest pitch as his dad patted a belly whose dress shirt was tucked firmly into pajama pants. Graham Pudowski was always professional.

"Oh, this is a highly amusing creation, sir. He wiggles! He bounces! He'll hold your phone! Mr. Takahashi, I'd wager that—Hello? Hello?" Dad stared at the suddenly blank screen in frustration. "Mum! Did you unplug my router again? I had Tokyo . . . and I need this contract."

"Baaaaaa!"

From nowhere, Gran's goat lunged at Barney with bleating fury. Before he could blink, it started chewing at his jacket the same way it did their lawn and most of the furniture.

"Come on! Get off!"

"Oh, hi, Barney!" Dad looked up absent-mindedly. "Good day?"

"Sure. It was fine." What else could Barney say about it?

Barney made a beeline for his upstairs bedroom, but too late.

"Barney?! Is it Barney I hear?" came Donka's voice from the kitchen. "Oh, happy birthday! Happy birthday! Yes yes yes! Come here!"

More than seventy years on earth and Barney's grandmother could still move like a wild boar defending its babies. Donka swung Barney around in a move that was part hug, part headlock, and her bulbous, wrinkled face planted a dozen kisses on him.

"This way, now. Eyes shut!" Donka commanded as she slid a ladle into her tool belt next to spare wiring, wrenches, and the dozens of other gadgets she used to keep the house together. "Graham! Come!" Barney heard the familiar sound of Dad scrambling to obey his own mother before he got a smack around the ears.

The pair led Barney into the kitchen. He already knew it was festooned with strings of extra salamis, multipacks of energy drinks and cheese doodles, and a handful of colorful birthday pennants, which were barely covering Donka's prized wall of black-and-white family photos. Gran loved a deal at an outlet superstore almost as much as she loved the old country, and the room had been done up for days in anticipation of the big party he had no idea how to call off.

"And now . . . ta-da for my lovely boy!" Donka cried before slamming a thick hat on his head. "Made with love from our own goat's wool!"

Barney felt the itch of his allergies already starting to creep in.

"And from me," Dad said. Barney heard a loud thump as his father inevitably banged his head on the low doorway. He cracked an eye open and saw Dad reaching back for *something*.

Barney had never genuinely thought he could get a B*Bot. He knew money was tight and had told himself he'd never ask—Dad had too much on his plate. But despite his best efforts, in this moment, his heart did flutter and his hope betrayed him as he fully opened both eyes and wondered if it could be, if there was any possible way that—

"Rock hammers?" Barney said.

"You always did love your rocks!" Dad beamed proudly.

"Yeah, I did . . . always . . . used to." Barney pulled the hat off and sniffed, smiling as best he could. Poor old Dad, always three years too late. "Sorry, Gran. But you know how the goat gets to my allergies."

"No no no." She shook her head. "No one in Pudowski family have allergy!"

"What about Uncle Boris?" Dad asked.

"He was possessed . . . by a demon in cashew!" she wagged a wise finger. "Now. What time your friends come, Barney? I cook all day." Donka ran across to the stove and began lifting lid after lid to unveil chicken hearts and sausage stews and her absolute favorite — shkembe, a soup made from lamb stomachs.

Barney's heart sank yet further. Poor Gran really had been cooking all day. If only he'd been brave enough to tell her he didn't want a party and that a slice of cake and dinner for three was fine by him. But then he'd have had to tell her why. And he couldn't bear the thought of telling his family that this — the house, the goat, the pajamas, the salamis hanging from the ceiling — *this* was the reason why he had no friends.

Barney loved his family more than anything, but in his quiet moments he wondered if he could ever make friends while he still lived in this house. Other kids had dogs and climbing frames in their front yards, not goats and lines of laundry. Other kids had Taco Tuesday, not tripe soup night. Other kids had living rooms with big TVs and plenty of couch space, not amateur storage units sitting among a jungle of wires. And because of this, Barney thought sadly as he looked into the kind, smiling faces of Gran and Dad, other kids have friends.

"The thing is," Barney said as he backed out of the room. "I mean . . . no one is coming."

"You ask and all say no?" Donka shook her head. "But everyone come to last party, remember? When you were six?"

How could he forget? When most kids turn six, they get a clown at their party or an ice-cream bar or bouncy castle. Barney got what his gran called a "celebratory extravaganza." Donka set up knife throwing, pin the tail on the goat — a real goat — a sausage-stuffed piñata, and half a dozen other insane activities. Several goat kicks and a small fire later found six-year-old Barney in his room as screaming kids were led away by irate parents. It was only a matter of time before friends stopped coming over to play permanently.

Dad's brow furrowed behind his glasses and his voice jerked Barney back to the present. "Son, we're a little worried about you," he said slowly. "You never go out or have any friends over. We thought it'd be good to invite the whole class over. Get the gang here! Get you in the swing of things!"

"I make food for all your buddies," Gran explained as the goat crept up between them and licked the wet ladle in her belt.

"I don't really *have* any—" Barney stopped. It was no use explaining the problem, only the solution. "You know, the kids probably just didn't read the invites. No one does paper anymore. They send messages . . . with their B*Bots."

Barney waited to see how it would land. Only the goat seemed convinced.

"Really?" Dad said. "You need a B*Bot to have a social life these days?"

"Yeah, Dad! Kind of!"

"No!" his father crossed his arms. "I don't want you addicted to some device. You should be out there . . . playing in the woods! Kicking around with a buddy! Get out there, Barn. Interact! You don't want to spend your whole life glued to a—"

Ping! Ping! Ping!

Dad's phone lit up with an international call signal, and he immediately got sucked back into his work. "Mr. Takahashi? No, of course, so glad to reconnect!"

Donka puckered up her face in disgust as Dad ran back to the office. "Bah!" she said. "The computers and phones and now these . . . *B*Bots*! It just a craze, and they cost so much money!"

Barney took his rock hammers and headed toward the door. "Yeah, yeah, you're right, Gran." He sighed. "It's just a waste of money. No big deal."

But then the doorbell rang. Barney opened the door slowly, expecting a new shipment of stock for his dad's business—a crate of wind-up rabbits or Halloween-themed eraser heads. But instead, what greeted him was an egg-shaped three-foot-tall box emblazoned with the Bubble logo. Barney's heart skipped a beat, and he jumped at the box.

"What? It can't be! Dad, you were kidding me!" he called as he frantically ripped the cardboard apart and began to uncover the egg-shaped object inside. "I knew you wouldn't just give me rock hammers. I knew it. I—Oh . . ."

Barney pulled the last shred of packaging off his present. It was a rock. A big, B*Bot-sized rock.

Rich popped out with his B*Bot's eye-cameras tracking Barney's every move. "Yo, I got the whole thing, bro!" he laughed. "It was hilarious, Barn. You thought it was a B*Bot! This one'll get a million views!"

"Let it go, Rich," Barney said, dropping the rock back into the box and letting the door swing loose behind him.

"Get out of here! You want I pour hot chicken fat down your pants?!" Donka shouted as the bully prankster hammed it up for his own camera. Gran shut the door and called up after Barney as he ascended to his room. "Barney! You no have your tripe soup!"

He shut his door and collapsed on his bed. It wasn't their fault; not really. They were trying their best. But in his heart, Barney knew they'd never really understand what it was like to be a kid in the twenty-first century. They didn't see how a child could be surrounded by people all day and yet be connected to no one.

Downstairs, the music of Zany Bogomil started pumping from the stereo for the party no kid would be caught dead at.

But as Barney lay in his room, chipping away at a rock and counting down the hours until his birthday was over, his family was embarking on the strangest of secret missions.

"B*Bot, B*Bot . . . not something useful like a snow shovel or a cordless drill!" Donka ranted as she tore across town in her pickup. As she careened around a corner, her son held on for dear life in the passenger seat.

"It's what he really wanted." Graham Pudowski sighed, thinking of his son home alone. "If his Mom were alive, she'd have known that . . ."

Donka was a woman of action. "If B*Bot is what he wants, we will make deal," she said, giving her son a sympathetic squeeze.

But within half an hour, the pair of them were

pressed up against the glass of the futuristic Bubble Store in town, pleading with the store manager, Bree. The Bubble Store employee looked harmless enough with her metallic red hair and ear piercings, and Donka tried everything she knew — she pleaded, she cursed, she sang, she flirted, she threatened, she bargained the goat, but nothing would sway Bree, who kept apologizing over and over, saying the store was closed and that even if it wasn't, B*Bots were so popular that there was now a three-month waiting list.

All seemed lost. Graham turned away, crushed, only to find a Bubble delivery van unloading in an alleyway. At the back of the van, half-hidden, sat a battered, dented box marked Return for Repairs . . .

CHAPTER 4
ABSALOM ACTIVATION

The next morning, Barney's vision went from blurred to razor sharp in about three seconds. It wasn't usual that he woke to the sight of his dad and gran leaning over him. Was the world ending?

"Uh . . . hey, guys." He rubbed the sleep from his eyes and inched backward on the bed. "Need something?"

"Happy late birthday, Barney," Dad said, pulling up a slightly smooshed but instantly recognizable box onto the bed.

"What? Dad . . . Dad, you got me one? A B*Bot?!"

"A real one this time," his dad said with a smile.

"Yeah, I can see! Thank you thank you thank you! And Gran!" Barney hugged them, then started tearing at the packaging and unveiling the pill-shaped bot underneath the cardboard that was . . . really pretty beat up.

"If you hurry, you can take it to school," Dad said, smiling proudly as he and Donka left the room.

"Here we go," Barney said, hardly daring to believe.

Barney reached out a hand and rested it on the B*Bot's front, just like he'd seen the girl do at the global launch — like he'd seen a hundred kids do as he scooted by the Bubble Store every weekend. But nothing happened. The bot stood lifeless.

Barney stared at the screen as its pinwheel icon began to spin. It's chest displayed "5 Percent Download Complete."

Five minutes passed. Then ten. "Come on!" Barney said before the screen updated with a *blip* . . . and read "4 Percent Download Complete." Confused, Barney took the bot in both hands and shook it as hard as he could. Then suddenly, it sprung to life.

"Hi, Insert-Registered-Name!" the machine declared in a flat voice. "I am your . . . I am your . . ."

"My B*Bot!" Barney shouted as it glitched.

"B-B-O-T. My Best Friend Out of the Box!"

Ping!

"I am Insert-Registered-Name's Best Friend Out of My Box! Insert-Registered-Name is my best friend," the B*Bot recited. "Please connect me to the Bubble Network."

"You're not online?" Barney said in confusion. "So how am I supposed to fix that?"

"No problem! I'll scan my database to found out how to do it."

"Oh, great, cool . . ." Barney breathed easy as it searched its help function.

Ping! "The answer to your question . . . is on the Bubble Network!" the bot said finally.

What in the heck was going on? This bot wasn't acting like any B*Bot he'd ever heard of, and despite owning a Bubble account with absolutely no devices synched, Barney knew how they were supposed to work.

"Please connect me to the Bubble Network, Insert-Registered-Name," the bot repeated.

"Stop. Stop saying that! It's not my name."

"No problem! Please select a name from my

internal database. Aadash . . . Aaron . . . Abraham . . . Absalom . . ."

"Absalom?" Barney repeated in confusion. How old a reference was that? Something was definitely wrong.

"Hi, Absalom! I am . . . Absalom's B*Bot!"

"No, no, no, no, no! My name is Barney."

"What is a Barney? I have only entries for the letter A. Shall I complete my download?"

"Yes . . . yes! Do that!"

"No problem," the little bot said. "Please connect me to the Bubble Network!"

"Oh, forget it, let's just cover the basics on the way," Barney said as he pulled on some clothes and headed for the door. His B*Bot sat on the bed, staring after him with a blank face. "You coming?"

It followed, but strangely. Down the stairs, the B*Bot rammed into the rails, then as Barney opened up the front door, it rushed out at full speed, swerving into the street. A delivery truck screeched to a halt, smacking into the bot, which rolled underneath.

"Sorry!" Barney called to the driver before shouting underneath to the malfunctioning machine,

"What are you doing? You walked under a truck! What about your traffic sensors?"

"Hi, Absalom!" the bot cheerily announced as it wiggled its body back toward the sidewalk. "What is a 'truck'? Is it an airplane? An ambulance? An alligator?"

"Come on. We've got to go to school."

The B*Bot stopped short again. "My solar battery function has not been uploaded," it said happily before completely collapsing into Barney's arms. Barney struggled to drag the lifeless form back inside, working up a sweat on the stairs, until he was finally able to pull it into his bedroom and drop it in the packaging's still-intact charging cradle.

With a short ping, the face on the B*Bot came alive again. "Hi, Absalom!"

"I'M BARNEY!" he shouted back. Maybe it would just need time to fully update and then it'd take his Bubble account info like it was supposed to. Hopefully. "How come you can't remember who I am? You're supposed to know *everything* about me!"

The bot pinged with a strange look of recognition. "I'm supposed to know *everything about you*," it repeated in its same cheery monotone.

"Just stay here and . . . learn stuff! I'll be back after school so we can do it right," said Barney. He ran out the door. From its charger, the B*Bot's eyes scanned the room. "Learn stuff . . . ," it repeated.

CHAPTER 5
CRUSHING IT

Barney ran home after a school day that seemed endless. Somehow, the drama surrounding everyone else's B*Bots was even more unbearable now that he had his own waiting at home. Noah had temporarily lost control of his B*Bot to another gamer after losing a tournament in *Undead Splatterfest 3*. This gave his opponent the ability to command Noah's bot to combo with his own and make an extra-impressive "multi-bot." But for Barney, the worst part was how he couldn't escape Noah's moans of losing his spot on the leaderboard. Meanwhile, Ava caught Savannah giggling at the paltry three people following the former's Science Squad channel. Ava shrugged it off with a smirk and a cutting remark, but Barney had seen the look of hurt on her face.

Maybe that was why Barney had done it. He pictured Savannah's hundreds of followers who watched her every move getting in Ava's head like they always had his own. So, in a moment where he finally felt like he could belong, he blurted, "I could follow your channel, Ava . . . I've got a B*Bot, too, now."

"Uh . . . okay," said Ava tentatively.

Barney had told himself not to overshare, to make sure the B*Bot was working properly before announcing it to the kids. But he had to do something, despite the fact that his profile was still downloading at home. Oh well, so he had mentioned he had a B*Bot. What was the worst that could happen? He was going to be bringing it to school, anyway. Things were different now. He didn't have to wait anymore to see if he might get a friend. He had one waiting for him upstairs.

But what he found as he sprinted to his room was less than friendly. His mattress was ripped open, stuffing lying everywhere. His books were blasted off the shelves and lying about, tattered and torn. His clothes, thrown out of the drawers, hung from every surface and stretched over the bedposts. And all that

37

remained of his underpants was a smoldering pile in the middle of the floor.

Barney picked up the decapitated head of his beloved childhood stuffed rabbit, Mr. Bunky, and heard the rhythm of Zany Bogomil from downstairs. He ran downstairs and found his gran bouncing around on top of the kitchen table with the B*Bot.

"Opa! Opa! Barney, I love new friend B*Bot! He's very funny!" Donka laughed.

"Hey! What did you do to my room?" Barney snapped off the radio.

"I have stayed here and learned stuff," the bot explained. "I now know everything about you. I know your underpants combust at a temperature of two hundred and thirty-two degrees Fahrenheit . . . seven degrees below the melting point of your inhalers!" It held up a pile of warped plastic that once supported Barney's lungs. "I know you own eleven socks and four books detailing the life of Bill the Bus. Now I am your Best Friend Out of the Box, Absalom!"

"No!" Barney shouted. "A friend does not go through your stuff or burn it or melt it . . . or dismember Mr. Bunky!"

"Removing Mr. Bunky's head required a breaking point of seven point six newtons," the bot reported. Barney yanked the bot toward the front hall.

Barney gave his gran an exasperated look. "The B*Bot has something wrong with it," he said.

A meat cleaver from Donka's toolbelt suddenly wiggled free, flying through the air until it clanked against the bot's shell, magnetically sticking in place. The bot wiggled out of Barney's grip and began spinning on the ground in some strange celebration.

"It look all right to me," Donka said.

"It's not meant to do that," Barney said flatly.

"I'm not meant to do that!" the bot screeched cheerily and released his magnetic pull on the cleaver so it shot through the air until it smashed a pickle jar to pieces.

"Maybe . . . turn it off and on again?" Donka said hopefully.

"No, it just doesn't work properly!" Barney shook his head.

"I fix it," said Donka, hefting the B*Bot in one hand and a drill in the other. "Pudowskis make do and mend!"

"What, no! You'll make it worse!" Barney cried, grabbing for the drill.

"Eh! Once I mend my own hernia with bread knife and vodka!" she declared.

It was too much. Barney wrestled the bot away from her. There was obviously a defect. It wasn't changing its skin or generating games or reaching out on the Bubble Network to make new friends with other kids. This bot had to go and *now*.

"People don't mend stuff anymore, Gran. They just take it back and —"

"Take it back?" She gasped, horrified. "You want I tell your father —"

"No!" This was exactly what Barney had hoped to avoid. Dad and Donka were trying their best, he knew that much. He couldn't bear to tell Dad it wasn't right, not just when Dad had finally got him the thing he wanted most in the whole world. Barney despaired — what was he going to do?

"Take it outside," said Donka, kindly. "Have fun with him."

Barney made a decision. He would deal with this himself — no need to involve Dad or Gran. Bubble was famous for their customer service—he was sure that if he explained it was defective, they could swap it out for a new one. He stuffed the remaining shreds of his bent packaging into his oversize school backpack and then dragged the giddy, glitching bot out into the street.

"Dikky dikky dakka dikky!" its autotuned voice hummed. Barney cringed as it called from behind him, "Where are we going, Absalom?"

"Um . . . nowhere . . ." Barney couldn't bring himself to tell the bot it was going back to the Bubble Store. "Just follow me."

As they headed down the street, the bot bopped along to his own singing, occasionally bumping into the odd mailbox or trashcan. "Hi, General Waste!" he cheerily said to a bin. "My friend Absalom and I are going to Um Nowhere to have some fun!"

"This is not fun, okay?" Barney snapped. "And you are *not* my friend."

"But I am your Best Friend Out of the Box!"

"Listen, friendship is a two-way street. I get to choose my friends." Barney stared at the bouncing, oblivious bot. "And I don't choose you, all right? No offense, but I have to swap you for a good one."

It kept singing the wacky song. After all this waiting and hoping, this was what Barney's B*Bot had to be? Everything about it was a disaster. Things couldn't possibly be worse.

"All right, y'all! This one's called the Seesaw Slammer!" came a familiar voice from across the otherwise deserted playground.

"Oh no!" Barney's stomach dropped as he saw Rich Belcher motioning Jayden and Alex into place on the playground equipment in the square's center. The bullies stood between Barney and the Bubble Store. Maybe there was some way around them?

Rich leaped off a slide as his lackies and their bots weighed down one side of the seesaw. He landed on the other and with a loud crack, the seesaw split into two. Immediately, Rich looked to his bot who was filming away. "Did you get that?"

"Zero views!" The bot bellowed as if it was something to be celebrated.

Too late, Barney realized he had pointed his malfunctioning B*Bot right at them.

"Dikky dikky dakka dikky!" Barney's bot sang as it flew across the square toward the trio. Out in the daylight, the bot looked more dysfunctional than ever. Rich's B*Bot was skinned with sunglasses and style to match his clothes. But Barney's was still just plain white — an unremarkable B*Bot singing a Bulgarian pop song no one had heard of.

"Woah, woah, woah! What is this?" Rich leaped from the seesaw, laughing. "A naked B*Bot?! I can see its ro-butt! Get it? Ro-butt?!?" His friends laughed right in time.

"I am Absalom's B*Bot!"

"You mean Barney?" Rich said looking up to where Barney sheepishly walked over.

"Rich, could you please give it back?" Barney tried to sound confident but nonthreatening. "I'm just taking it back to the store."

"Yeah, sure Barn. Take it," Rich said but then stepped in front of the bot as the whole crew circled around it. "But first, you gotta do something for me?"

"Excuse me?"

"Your gran called the school to get me in trouble for the rock bit. That's on you, dude. So I'm gonna need you to cheer us up, Barney. Do something funny. Give me some fresh content for my channel." Jayden and Alex laughed behind him, their bots joining in like a chorus of jackals.

"No way, Rich. Just give him back," Barney said. He didn't owe this kid a thing.

"Just get into the rhythm of this song, Pudowski," Rich sneered. "Seems just like your style."

The B*Bot danced amid the other kids, still humming along to the Zany Bogomil tune. "Dikky dikky dakka dikky!" its voice rang out on a loop.

They all stood like that for a tense moment. Barney was rooted to the ground, and his resolve was getting to Rich almost as much as the song droning on and on from the clueless bot they'd surrounded. Finally, the bully snapped. He stepped aside and slapped Barney's B*Bot as hard as he could, pushing it out of their circle and toward the ground.

"Why did you hit me?" the bot asked cheerfully as it rose up.

"Because I don't like you, derp-droid!" Rich shouted.

"I don't like *you*, derp-droid!" the B*Bot repeated as if it were a game and then flipped his little white arm out and slapped Rich full-on across the face. The bully stumbled to the ground as they all went silent in shock.

"Ow!" Rich cried, holding his reddening cheek. "What's wrong, you dumb bot!" He rushed up and tried to shove Barney's bot, but it only glided a few inches in the air. And then it shoved back. Hard.

Rich flew over the broken seesaw and skidded into the sandbox, his pristine jacket deflating as dirt rubbed in. Barney gasped and a giggle escaped his lips involuntarily. *It just hit Rich Belcher!* Rich was stammering now. "But . . . but . . . B*Bots can't shove!"

"Incorrect," Barney's Bot said with a slightly menacing smile. "I can shove with a compressive force capacity of twenty-nine pounds per square inch. Let me show you!"

"You do it, and I'm gonna destroy you!" Rich cried nervously.

"Great!" Barney's Bot began to chase Rich around the park with gleeful shouts of "I'm going to destroy you! I'm going to destroy you!" Barney found himself laughing as the bullies scattered, their bots all "Contacting local law enforcement" at Rich's high-pitched request.

"Is this FUN, Absalom?" The bot asked Barney, hearing him laugh.

"Yes, I — no, but —" Barney felt a wild surge of adrenaline as the bullies scrambled up fences and slides to get away from the bot. This was wrong, yet it *was* fun.

But when the bot cornered a screaming Rich and started playfully pulling on his head, Barney realized he had to do something. Rich was annoying, but he didn't deserve the same fate as Mr. Bunky.

"Stop! You can't pull his head off!" Barney shouted, running forward.

"Okay, Absalom," said the bot with a ping of a learning chime. "I cannot pull his head off."

Barney watched as his basic bot rolled back over, still bouncing as if it were singing the Zany song. "That was fun, Absalom!"

But Rich was climbing down from the fence and straightening his jacket, a menacing look in his eye. "You are DEAD MEAT, Pudowski!" Jayden and Alex advanced from opposite sides.

"Okay, we have to run — now!" Barney said as he grabbed the bot.

Whooping with the thrill of escape, Barney pounded away over the fence and up the hill, his

B*Bot right behind. His asthma meant he always lost his breath quicker than other kids, but the pure adrenaline and sense of adventure made it barely noticeable. They flew through the bushes at the park's edge, giggling and laughing, and down into a ditch where Barney collapsed, convulsing and wheezing.

He stopped, concerned, when the bot started making a strange noise. But after a second, he realized it was just parroting his own asthma laugh, and he fell about laughing again with his new partner in crime.

"That was awesome!" Barney beamed before reconsidering. "But it was also kind of terrible. But awesome! I mean, you can't hit people, especially Rich Belcher . . . but you hit Rich Belcher! How is that even possible? B*Bots are supposed to have mega safety controls and stuff."

"Incorrect," the bot said. "I have no mega-safety-controls-and-stuff. The settings have not been uploaded. So let us go and swap me for a good one."

"Wait," Barney said, looking at the bot with new eyes. "Maybe we can . . . I mean . . ."

"Freeze!" shouted a voice from a loudspeaker on the street behind them. A series of siren chirps followed as Barney and the bot turned to see a policeman staring them down from his squad car. "Put your hands where I can see them," the cop called before speaking into his vest radio. "Yeah, I think it's him . . . white, two-foot tall, plastic shell . . . tell the folks at Bubble they better prepare the *crusher*."

CHAPTER 6
JAILBREAK

The brightly lit inside of the Bubble Store felt far less exciting when Barney was in trouble. He crouched low with an arm around his B*Bot as the circle of people arguing over "what had to be done" grew. Dad tried his best to stand between the angry cop, Donka, and Barney. And trying to referee was Bree, the store manager whose customer service niceness seemed ready to break at any moment.

"I'm sorry, but as the Bubble Corporation's senior representative here, this is making no sense to me," Bree said. "Our B*Bots are friends, not criminals."

"That thing is violent, uncontrollable, and highly dangerous," said the officer. "It assaulted a child!"

"Okay, great. Let me look into that," Bree said, calmly waving over a number of idle Bubble Buddies from across the sales floor.

"It didn't assault Rich," Barney spoke up.

"I hit Rich Belcher! It was awesome but terrible but awesome!" the B*Bot joyfully admitted.

"Barney, were you fighting?" Dad turned to look at the pair.

"No . . ." Barney was unsure how to answer. "He was just mimicking what we said to him . . . what *I* said to him. He's my bot!"

"According to our records, it has no registered owner," Bree said, swiping her finger down a BubblePad.

"Oh, we paid plenty for it," Donka said firmly. "I give all my funeral money to that man in the alley."

Bree looked Dad dead in the eye. "Sir, did you obtain this bot illegally?"

"See?!" the cop cried. "This thing is criminal through and through. It needs to go to the crusher or I'll be forced to close this whole store!"

"Fine," Bree relented. "One crushing coming up."

The officer took the B*Bot by its arm. Barney looked at its sweet blank face as it was carried away. He panicked. All of a sudden, having a B*Bot that didn't work right didn't seem so bad.

"No!" he cried. "It's my birthday present!" He grabbed the other end of the B*Bot and a tug-of-war ensued. But it was no use; the B*Bot slipped from his grip, swatting the cop in the face as it went. Soon, Bree's team of Bubble Buddies were leading it up the escalator.

"Adios, Absalom! Arrivederci! Auf wiedersehen! Will crushing be fun?" the bot called to Barney.

"Come on, son. We better let it go," Dad said.

But Barney wouldn't have it. This was his only chance.

He rushed up the escalator, scanning the massive Bubble Store. On each new open floor, translucent domes housed themed B*Bots, showing off a variety of features. One was fully dedicated to a Luchador wrestling ring where bots skinned themselves as the masked wrestlers and grappled to applause. Another showed off educational programs bots could offer preschoolers as they morphed into woodland critters from within a foam-lined forest set. A third dome, the kind Noah Lee would frequent, had scores of bots locked in an eternal space laser battle with awed kids watching on. But nowhere did Barney see *his* bot.

Then, for a split second, Barney caught a glimpse of a Bubble Buddy employee pushing something through a door marked Staff Only. Barney snuck up behind a rack of ninety-dollar power cords, and when no one was watching, he followed along into the back corridors.

Barney snuck down the gray, dingy hallway until he came upon a massive chomping trash compactor. All around, a scattered graveyard of defective Bubble product boxes littered the dirty floor. The employee put Barney's Bot on a conveyor belt, turned a switch, and headed out a far door. Barney jumped in just in time.

"Hi, Absalom! Happy birthday!" the bot said when it spotted Barney. Then it pulled Barney into a tight hug on the conveyor belt.

"Shhhhh! What are you doing?!" Barney called in a panic as the conveyor belt inched closer to the compactor.

"Waiting to be crushed. A friend must stick within six feet of his friend. Let's get crushed together!"

"No!" Barney whisper-shouted. How could he get

through to the bot? Then he remembered that the bot would only truly understand him if he spoke in As. "Being crushed is *not* fun! It means smooshed . . . flattened . . . ah . . . a . . . annihilated!"

"Annihilated." The bot registered. "Not fun." He rolled them off just in time.

Barney sighed in relief and motioned toward the exit. "Shh! We gotta get out of here!"

"Hey, kid! What are you doing back here!"

They'd been spotted! Barney and the B*Bot grabbed hands and sprinted back inside the store. The second they crossed beyond the door and onto the sales floor, Barney could see a red alert chime on every BubblePhone attached to the belt of each Bubble Buddy. They all turned to look his way. This was going to be impossible.

"Okay," Barney said, looking around. "We have to—WHAT ARE YOU DOING?!" The bot was wandering cheerily toward the escalators, totally out in the open.

"We gotta get out of here!" it yelled back at him.

"No!" Barney shouted as it descended out of sight. "Come back!"

Barney sprinted for the escalators, almost knocking another kid down, straightening up in time to *see the bot coming up the other side?!*

"You said 'come back'!" the B*Bot said cheerily.

Groaning, Barney spun around and went back up the down escalator, bumping into the same kid and moving at about half a mile an hour.

Barney pursued the bot through the Bubble Store as the Bubble Buddies fanned out, combing the place like a security team. "Tres, dos, unooooooooooo!" cried a referee bot as Barney and his glitchy companion broke up a match in the store's wrestling ring.

Panicking, Barney grabbed his B*Bot and dove across into another show dome's laser fight. They ran through the projected battleground, the other bots bowing down in awe when Barney's bot's blank body failed to register all the hits it was taking, proclaiming him "The Invincible One." Emerging to find Bubble Buddies on either side, they slid down the first escalator level past Bubble Buddies shouting into headsets, and the bot dove headfirst into the preschool forest with Barney close on his heels.

They scrambled low on their bellies as toddlers wobbled all around. Barney's backpack snagged a strap on a passing preschooler bot. It turned slowly, its squirrely skin smiling with digital buckteeth.

"I'm Sally Squirrel!" sang the bot. "It's potty time! Number one or number two! Let's learn where we pee and poo!"

"No! Shhhh! Power down! Power down!" Barney whispered as he struggled to untangle himself from it.

Bree's voice rang out over the store's intercom. "To the middle schooler hiding in Preschool Forest: We see you! You are surrounded! Come out now and hand over the B*Bot!"

The lights turned up all the way. The crowd of little bots parted. This was it. Barney was cooked. He had to give up the bot to be destroyed.

Walking out into view, everyone stared at Barney as he held the lifeless white machine in both arms. His dad rushed to his side, but Barney just handed it over to Bree, expression stony. "It's okay," he said. "They can take it."

In the parking lot, Donka waited by the family's ramshackle truck. "How dare they?" she said. "Calling my boy a criminal! We paid for B*Bot with cash in hand! It fair and square!"

"Let's talk about it at home, Mom," Dad said as Barney climbed into the back and nestled himself in among Gran's piles of boxes and tools. She turned the radio up as they rode back home, but Barney only stared into the backpack he held in his lap. And at the treasure he had inside.

"Hi, Absa—!"

"Shhhh! Keep quiet," Barney whispered. "I can't believe that worked. Poor little Squirrel Bot, but at least now I can take you home."

The bot stared up at him quizzically. "But you choose your friends, and you did not choose me."

"I do, okay? I choose you," Barney said. "I'll find a way to fix you. I can . . . teach you, you know? I'll teach you how to be my friend."

"Okay, Absalom."

"First things first," Barney said. "Absalom may be my registered name, but my friends call me Barney. Got that?"

"And my friends call me . . ." The bot scanned his scattered memory banks and displayed a long serial number: RONB1NTSATSCO. "Ron Binscatsco!"

"Nice to meet you then, *Ron*."

"Nice to meet you . . . Barney." The newly named B*Bot stared up at its owner and, for the first time, really seemed to see him.

CHAPTER 7
THE BUBBLE CODE

From that moment on, Ron was maybe the only secret in the universe hidden from the Bubble Corporation. At their Silicon Valley headquarters, the company that created the worldwide phenomenon was celebrating its total dominance of the personalized friend market.

Deep inside the executive offices of the Bubble Dome, Andrew Morris and Marc Wydell looked out onto a massive LED sign that had been ticking upward since the B*Bot global launch that summer. Andrew stood on his toes with anticipation while Marc shambled about in the office he almost never visited except for moments like this.

Just past ten o'clock, the numbers on the sign finally crossed over into a one and eight zeroes.

"One hundred million!" Andrew shouted in a rare moment of astonishment. "One hundred million units sold!"

"Well, we made one hundred million new friends," Marc corrected. "All helping kids connect, meet each other, interact . . ."

". . . and all through their B*Bots! Through our servers!" Andrew jumped in. "Making friends face-to-face? So last three millennia. Some of these kids are checking in with the bots one hundred times a day, plus eleven times overnight. We've finally done it. We've ended sleep!"

Marc looked at a datapad and furrowed his brow. "The algorithm may need adjusting then. That's a little invasive."

"Bah!" Andrew waved his partner off. "Think of the data we'll be able to harvest in a year. We'll know what the next generation is dreaming about."

"That's not the point of the tech, Andrew. *I* designed this stuff . . ."

"Starting in *my* garage, Marc . . ."

"It's for making friends!"

"Yeah, making them into dollars. If our share price

goes any higher, we'll have to give it a spacesuit."

"Excuse me, Mr. Morris?" An assistant from the PR department snuck her head in the door. "We're going to need your input on what to do about this B*Bot hitting incident. The press are asking."

Andrew turned with an irritated look. "Hitting incident?" he said with a raised eyebrow. "I'm unaware of what this is."

"Well, it's difficult to explain, sir, and reports are varied. We've got Bree from store #1311 on the line here who can explain better." The assistant handed a BubblePad over to the cofounders, and Bree waved hello with a nervous look.

"What happened?" Marc asked.

"Today an unregistered B*Bot model attacked both a twelve-year-old boy and a local police officer," Bree said.

"It hit a cop?!" Andrew shouted.

"And a child," the store employee stressed.

"It hit a cop! We can't put that on the box!"

"No, no, that's not right. That's not possible," Marc took over. "B*Bots are incapable of violence. My algorithm ensures that no . . ."

"Maybe you should watch the footage," Bree explained and swiped over. The BubblePad then replayed the scene on the floor of the Nonsuch store where Barney's bot broke the tug-of-war and struck the officer.

Marc shook his head. "I'd better look into that."

"You think, Marc?" Andrew said. "I mean, what if someone gets injured by one of these things? I, for one, could not live with what that would do to our share price."

"It shouldn't be a problem, sirs," said Bree on screen. "We performed a complimentary in-store crushing as soon as the issue was brought to light."

"Good." Andrew Morris turned away and stared back at the counter, which had already turned over to one hundred million and one. "Because if *that* B*Bot was still out there, we'd be toast."

CHAPTER 8
FRIENDSHIP 1.0

Barney had never thought about what friendship was until he had to explain it to someone else, but he found that he had plenty of opinions on the matter. The evening after their close call at the Bubble Store, Barney and his bot created a safe space to explore the idea in the chicken shed out back behind the Pudowski household.

Cobbled together by Donka out of old sheet metal and leftover plywood, the shed was connected to an even older chicken coop by a dingy ramp that ran the length of the backyard. Since most of that year's chicken flock had already been converted into feet-first lunches for Barney, it was easy to clear the shack of stragglers and set up a living space for Ron.

On one end of the tiny room, Barney hung a

bulletin board he'd pulled down from the house and, bit by bit, began a vision board to teach Ron everything he could on How to Be My Friend.

"A bunch of your code is missing, right?" Barney said as he set the board into place.

"The settings have not been uploaded," Ron confirmed.

"So, I'm gonna teach you to be my friend, and then you can come to school . . ."

"What is a friend, Barney?" Ron asked on their first night at the board.

"That's easy," said Barney, though he was suddenly at a loss for words. "A friend is a . . . person who . . . er . . . likes . . . is always . . . I . . ."

"A-person-who-er-likes-is-always-I! Okay. Now I am your best friend," Ron said and turned toward the door.

"Come back! There's a lot more, Ron." Barney, laughing, pulled him back into the shed and fitted him with the wool-knit hat his gran made for him, despite his allergies. And so began Ron's education, as Barney added Post-its to the Friendship Board.

Barney brainstormed sticky note after sticky note with any category of friendship knowledge he could

think of. Likes! Dislikes! Future goals! Every idea
birthed a rule. Every rule had examples. But some of
these examples contradicted the rule, and some of the
rules didn't make much sense. Before long, the entire
board was covered in notes, cards, and connecting string
to make the whole idea of being a friend more tangible
to Ron. Barney was constantly adding extensions and
crossings out and specific notations.

"Know Everything About Me" read one section. It
listed attributes like hair color or the gap in Barney's
teeth he could whistle through, alongside rules about
how to describe someone. But after Ron described his
eyes as "the color of goat droppings," Barney was
forced to add an exception: "But Don't Body Shame
Me!" And when Ron started criticizing his height,
Barney crossed out "Know Everything About Me" and
replaced it with "Like Everything About Me." Much
better.

But the shed lessons were nothing compared to
the field research. Tiptoeing through Donka's kitchen,
Barney shared how to make his favorite foods. Then,
as they snuck around Nonsuch after school each day,
Barney showed him the way to make a perfect pour

from the slushy machine at the gas station or how to track the rock formations within the cliffs by the river. Barney never realized how much of an expert he could be until he had someone around who needed endless explanations.

By night, they went over Barney's likes and dislikes in detail. The broad strokes were easy for Ron, but nuance took time. Alongside "Like What I Like" came a list of the good (rocks, chess, Pac-Man, butter on its own, Donka's cheese banitsas) and the bad (possums, musicals, school generally, and the Friendstop, specifically). More important, Barney stressed for Ron to "Be on My Side" (followed with "But Don't Hit People, Even Rich" and "Don't Burn My Underpants").

With each new day came navigation tutorials — Barney fitting Ron with a compass dangling from a cap and a map, then watching half-cringing, half-giggling as Ron powered through the streets and over roads and across bridges, exploring the town and never remembering any of it.

Barney and Ron also talked about how to be more like other B*Bots, so Ron could fit in at school. Ron tried to stick to the simple rules that fully downloaded

B*Bots followed. "Rule number one," he'd state. "Always stay within six feet of Barney."

"Unless I say not to," Barney corrected.

"Received. I will never stay within six feet of you," Ron updated.

"No! It's sometimes yes and sometimes no," Barney shook his head. "Like, if I need space or if I've had a bad day or . . ."

Ron let loose a series of pings. "Sometimes . . . never . . . need space . . . bad day . . . always six feet!" He ended by tumbling over onto his side, sending Barney into a fit of hysterics.

As their first week together flew by, Barney almost forgot about the other kids in his class. It was easier to be invisible at school when Barney knew he had someone he could open up to back home, and having something to look forward to made recess all the more bearable. He noticed a gradual change in Ron, too—the bot was forming more and more opinions.

"Okay, so my allergies . . . there's a lot of them," Barney said, ticking off the list on his fingers as they were holed up under an overpass one evening. "Goats, wool, goat's wool, salami, squirrels . . . seriously I can't get near a squirrel. I'm basically allergic to *life*. That's why I was always into rocks as a kid."

"That is sad and also tragic," Ron said.

"You have to like the same things as me!" Barney teased. "What do you even like . . . electricity?"

"Electricity is better than rocks."

"Electricity isn't even a thing!" Barney laughed. "It has no mass!"

"Still better than rocks," Ron reported back, throwing one at Barney.

All the while, the Friendship Board got bigger and bigger and messier and messier. The shed became their own little world, the board their secret project. Oftentimes their lessons were a failure, but weirdly these seemed even more fun than the successes. Barney spent half his day rolling around the floor giggling, and the other half thinking up new things to try with Ron. Everything outside of those four homemade walls fell away. No one, not his teachers, not Noah or Savannah or Ava or Rich, not even Dad and Donka, knew about what they were doing, and that made it even more special — it was theirs alone, Barney's and Ron's.

Even when Dad made his way out to the shed to

attempt to connect over a game of chess, Barney just turned him away. He kept Ron and their friendship locked up tight in that shed. Who cared if it looked like he was playing in there by himself all day?

That Sunday night, they posted up on a hillside overlooking town, their backs to a giant Bubble Corporation receiver tower.

"List Friends," Ron said, surprising Barney.

"Um, next question?" Barney laughed nervously. "I'm not actually unpopular, you know . . . That would mean they know I exist."

"List Relations," the bot continued.

"I've got Dad, Gran . . . and some great uncles I've never met." Barney stopped again. But he had to talk about it. "There was Mom, too, of course, but she died when I was two. And then Dad moved us out here. It doesn't make me sad exactly, because I can't remember her. But it did make things hard for him."

"She was returned to the facility?" Ron asked.

"I guess. No receipt." Barney reached up to scratch the back of his neck, a nervous habit.

"Scratches neck fourteen point five times a day," pinged the B*Bot.

"What are you doing?"

"I am learning about my friend."

Barney laughed.

"Please slap my hand to show we are bonding," Ron said with a raised flap.

Barney swung out a high five, but Ron powered down. "You went to sleep?!"

"No, it was a move," said Ron, straightening up and smiling. Barney laughed — he'd never had a special handshake before. He was excited, amped up at the feeling of having a friend to share moments like this with at last. He shoved Ron playfully, but maybe it was too hard, because the B*Bot started rolling straight down the hillside.

"Ron! Sorry!" Barney yelled while chasing after the increasingly speedy bot. "Hold on . . . stop! You're about to crash!"

It was too late. Ron rolled like a bowling ball straight down the hill, across a path, and through the shrubbery of a nearby backyard. Barney raced after just behind, but when he peered through the hole in the bush, he saw more than just his fallen comrade.

He saw Savannah Meades, too.

CHAPTER 9
FRIENDSHIP 2.0

Savannah's yard was every bit as flawlessly curated as her photo feed. Sparkling fairy lights lined every bush in the hedge surrounding her pool, lit up in a stunning shade of ocean blue. She lounged on a deck chair poolside, her B*Bot standing beside her like a cabana waiter, as she meticulously adjusted the filter on its camera.

"Okay, key light . . . Malibu filter . . . perfect." She flicked her hair back and planted a surprised expression on her face. "Oh, hey, guys! Just caught me chilli—AHHH!"

Ron burst through the hedge and landed in the pool, spinning upside down in a unicorn float, dragging the fairy lights around and around.

"Afloat . . . aquatic . . . activist . . . actor . . . ," he

70

said in a garbled, underwater voice.

"What is that?!" Savannah jumped to her feet in a panic as Barney stumbled through the bush. "It sounds like a giant snake or . . . an evil clown! They live in the woods; their heads go all the way round!"

Barney's lungs were on fire, nose red and breath wheezing. He struggled in his backpack to find his inhaler, finally taking a long pump, and then coughed. "Hey . . . Savannah . . . just been . . . running a bit . . . nice pool." Then he realized where his friend had landed. "Ron!"

He tried lifting the B*Bot out of the pool, but each time he got a hand on it, Ron would slip around again and bob up and down. With a *zap*, the backyard lights went out as Ron accidentally pulled a plug.

"You've ruined my aesthetic!" Savannah cried. "And since when did you have a B*Bot?"

Barney huffed again as he finally got his pal up from the water and onto the pool deck. He took another pull of his inhaler, and the pair collapsed into a deflating unicorn float.

"And hold on a sec . . . why has he not friended me?" Savannah swiped through her massive Bubble contact list extra fast just to make sure she hadn't been snubbed.

Savannah's B*Bot approached Ron from the other side of the pool. "Would you like to friend @theSavannahMeades?" it asked expectantly.

"Oh, it's okay." Barney sat up. "He can't really make friends or change his skin or . . . any of the Bubble stuff, really. He's useless at all that . . ."

"Can't make *friends*? Barney, don't say your weirdness has rubbed off on him. Making friends is, like, what he's *for*. If he can't do that he's, like, literally pointless."

"#Landfill," said her B*Bot, backing away.

"I am *for* making friends?" Ron asked. "How do I make friends for Barney?"

"Forget it, Ron. It's fine." Barney shrugged.

"Seriously?" Savannah stared at them. "You share stuff about him. Pictures of his food or his wake-up routine . . . You know, *content*! You search for people who know him or like the same stuff as him. You show them pictures, and then you get comments and likes and invites, and then — *Boom!* — you've made friends. It's, like, the only thing that matters."

"Does Barney need to make friends?" Ron was entirely focused on Savannah.

"Well, yeah!" she scoffed. "Or fun fact: He will not survive middle school."

Barney finally worked up the strength to push Ron back through the hole in the hedge. "Savannah, please don't tell anyone about this! I've got to keep him a secret!"

They rushed back through the hedge and ran dripping into the fresh night air, sticking much closer than six feet apart. Barney kept pumping his inhaler into his lungs as Ron pinged away in thought. It was just enough noise for them to drown out the sound of Savannah leaning over her B*Bot on the other side of the fence and saying, "Please tell me you got all of that."

Even though he was cold and shivering, Barney carried Ron home. But he couldn't bring himself to leave his friend in the lonely shed out back, so Ron ended up bunking under his bed.

Barney toweled him off and lay staring at the tiny lamp at his bedside table. He'd never told anyone that he was still afraid of the dark.

"Mind if I leave it on?"

Ron didn't reply at first. "I am literally pointless," he finally said.

"What?"

"I cannot make friends for you."

"Yeah, well, I'm not so great at that, either. You should see me during recess. It sucks. I stand there every day on my own at the edge of the yard, just hoping a few people will want to share a bench with me. But why would they? The last time any of them came to my house, we set fire to some of them."

"But not their underpants?" Ron asked.

Barney heard a zap and a shout from below—Dad was having computer troubles again. The light flickered, then turned off. Barney tried desperately to turn it back on but it wouldn't work.

"Guess I'll just leave it off. Goodnight, Ron."

Unseen by Barney, Ron projected his digital version of the Friendship Board onto the underside of the bed. Beneath "Know Stuff About Me," he added a new card—"Doesn't Like the Dark." Ron paused, thinking, then his body glowed a bit brighter, like a nightlight.

Up above, Barney smiled, drifting off to a peaceful sleep.

CHAPTER 10
CHECKING IN AT NONSUCH MIDDLE SCHOOL

The sun came up Monday morning, and Barney clung to the worry that everyone at school would know about Ron before too long. Now that he'd had Ron all to himself, the thought of sharing his friend in an endless stream of likes and selfies and status updates felt . . . wrong all of a sudden.

But Barney shouldn't have been worrying about that. He should have been worrying about the fleet of Bubble vans that were suddenly, almost invisibly, parked on every corner in Nonsuch.

Regardless, Barney woke up that morning and snuck Ron down to the shed and pressed his pal into their sacred space.

"Ron, you have to hide," he said. "You're just not

ready yet. I'm sorry. But I'll be back soon!"

The door closed, and as the B*Bot sat in the dimly lit space, it scanned their wall of friendship lessons and said, "But there are no friends in the shed."

The rest of the morning went in two very different directions.

While Barney was settling into homeroom after first bell, Ron was gathering a raft of Barney-centric supplies from around the Pudowski household: maps, food, signage, inhalers, and framed photographs. While Barney chewed his pencil over a pop quiz in pre-algebra, Ron rolled through a construction site and tossed buttered toast at people while calling, "I am sharing Barney's breakfast! Do you 'like' it?" While Barney doodled in his notebook during a history lecture, Ron approached an old woman at a bus stop with his best friend's naked baby picture. "Would you like to comment on this picture, old woman?" he said cheerfully. "Come to my secret shed for more!" And by the time Barney was trying to figure out what lunch to buy, Ron pushed open the doors at a local biker bar. "I'm gonna be late! My pants are on backward!" he said as he danced for the assembled bikers. "That was

Barney's wake-up routine!"

The recess bell rang at Nonsuch Middle School, and the hallways again flooded with B*Bots, lifting from their charging cradles where they waited for their owners to finish class. "You have six new likes . . . you have two new messages . . . ," the corridors echoed. But Barney couldn't hear any of it. He went into panic mode when he rolled up to his locker to find Ron covered in dirt smudges and waving with a huge digital grin across his faceplate.

"Ron! What are you doing here?!" He rushed up, trying to cover the B*Bot with his hands.

"There are no friends in the shed," Ron said. "I am *for* making friends. So I made many Friend Requests!"

Before Barney could reply, Noah Lee strode up. "Yo, Barn, you got a B*Bot?" he said. "Looks like he's seen some battle, dude. Right on."

"Uh . . . thanks."

A clique of art students and their paint-spattered B*Bots stared at them and whispered, "Wow. That's so minimalistic. Like a blank canvas."

In fact, everyone seemed to be noticing Ron . . .

and liking him? Maybe Barney's worries were misplaced. Maybe this would be all right after all.

"Recess will not suck today," Ron said, pulling him by the arm. "You will now have friends to share a bench with you."

The B*Bot dragged his friend onto the playground and pointed to the Friendstop. On its bench sat the strangest group of people Barney had ever seen. A woman older than Donka rested on a walker, half asleep. A hairy biker who towered over the swings and slides. An old homeless man petted at a squawking parrot. And . . . was that a baby?

"You have five new friends, Barney!" Ron beamed. "I did a search for them. Shayne rides on a hog and believes there is a secret lizard government beneath Disneyland. He will be your friend if he can stay in the shed."

"Barney bro!" the biker called out. "Don't worry. It's only for a year . . . two tops."

"Oh no . . . oh no no no . . ." Barney began to hyperventilate and reached for his inhaler.

Ron continued the tour of "friends" by explaining each one's social connection to Barney. There was the homeless man the B*Bot had "shared Barney's breakfast with" who was clearly hoping for a free lunch, too. On his shoulder perched a parrot, which belonged to the Pudowskis' neighbor Mrs. Baxter, tapped because "you share one friend in common: Mrs. Baxter!" The elderly woman was stammering as Ron noted she shared interests with Barney like "my purse, my watch . . . whatever you want just let me go!" And then there was the infant chewing on a printed copy of Barney's baby photo.

"Meet friend number five!" Ron said as he rolled the kid into Barney's personal space. "This tiny bald man likes your picture so much, he is eating it!"

Barney spun around in a cold sweat. But suddenly, he realized it wasn't just his new "friends" surrounding him. All the kids from school and their B*Bots had gathered around and were cheering on the circus Ron had created.

"This is like a rave!" Noah called out. "What did you call this little dude again?"

"Who?" Barney asked, patting the baby on its back. "Ron?"

"Yeah!" cried Noah, who then started to chant,

"Ron! Ron! Ron! Ron!" All the kids clapped along. Even Shayne the biker shouted with them. Barney was forgotten.

"There he is! Logan!" came a woman's cry so loud it cut the chant short. A teary-eyed mother rushed to Barney's side and plucked the baby out of his hands. "Oh, my baby! My poor baby!"

"I'm sorry!" Barney tried to explain. "I didn't know he would do this. He's just trying to help."

Just then, a meaty hand grabbed onto Barney's shoulder, *hard*. "I'll help you, Pudowski," called the gravelly voice of Mr. Cleaver. "Help you right to the principal's office."

CHAPTER 11
UNLOCKED

"Savannah?" Barney was shocked to find his classmate sitting in the lobby of the office, shaking with excitement. "What's going on?"

"It's Bubble!" she said. "They loved my post — they wanted to know all about it!"

"What post?"

Savannah's B*Bot projected an image of Ron slipping around the pool in the unicorn float. "Twenty thousand friends love 'B*Bot Goes Pool Crazy!'" the bot said.

Barney's stomach dropped. "Bubble knows," he said to himself. "But where are they?"

"They're on their way," Savannah said. Then she did something she'd never done — she *hugged Barney.* "You're such an actual weirdo, Barney, it's like almost cool!" But all Barney felt was afraid.

On the playground, Ron was probably in a tighter spot than his friend. The crowd around the B*Bot's flimsy friend group hadn't broken up, but no one was quite sure what to do except marvel at the weird little bot who somehow couldn't connect with the other kids' Bubble-built companions.

Then Rich Belcher walked up.

"It's you, isn't it?" the bully said, sneering at Ron. "You're not new at all. You're the crazy broken dude who punched me. How'd you do it?"

"I have no mega-safety-controls-and-stuff!" Ron replied.

"Hey, bros!" Rich called to his cronies. "This thing's nuts! Safety settings . . . parental controls . . . account limits . . . everything's turned off!"

"And that's how come he hit you?" Alex laughed. "Dude, I want mine like that, too. Then it can hit me!" Alex wasn't the sharpest kid.

"If we could unlock our B*Bots, it'd be a game changer . . ." Rich's eyes went wide at the idea.

"I could download all the R-rated movies I want!" Jayden said.

"Wait, seriously?" Noah walked over with his gamer B*Bot in tow. "You think I could get like ten thousand megabucks? Unlimited in-game purchases?"

"And I could get access to every piece of code in the Bubble system!" Ava said, pushing her way to the front of the crowd.

"You guys are all thinking too small" Rich said as he fiddled with the Wi-Fi settings of his own B*Bot. "I could prank the whole world! All I need is to connect mine to this Ron . . . Come on and open up that bandwidth!"

Ping! One touch was all it took then. And suddenly, the kinks in Ron's code that let him break Bubble's control were uploaded and overwriting the safety settings in any B*Bot in range still connected to Bubble's global network. The company couldn't control what they did anymore. Every kid in Nonsuch who wanted to break the rules had a best friend without limits.

Barney couldn't hear the cries of joy from where he sat in the principal's office. He just heard the tick of the clock and the beating of his own heart as he waited for the ax to drop. Staring across the desk at him was

the principal, flanked by Bree and two other Bubble
Buddies who loomed like government agents with grim
expressions.

"Pudowski, what is going on?" said the principal.

"Where is the bot?" chimed in Bree. She brought
up a video clip on her BubblePad and hit play on the
security footage from that day in the Bubble Store.
Barney and Ron crouched low in the Preschool Forest,
the boy laughing as they hid Ron in his backpack,
and the B*Bot mimicking the sound. "We know the
malfunctioning unit escaped crushing, and I won't
let it get away again on my watch. Bubble Buddies
are surrounding the campus to find this thing. Even
Andrew Morris and Marc Wydell have seen this
footage, and they're very anxious to examine this piece
of equipment, Mr. Pudowski."

The cofounders of Bubble knew who Barney
was? He marveled at the idea for a moment before a
sinking feeling of dread hit. His secret was out now.
What exactly would they do with Barney's weird,
dysfunctional B*Bot? And how much trouble was he
himself in?

"He's just out on the playground . . . making

friends," Barney finally relented. "He's not causing trouble at all. You'll see."

The secretary burst in at that very moment. "You better get out here. There's trouble in the hallway . . . on the playground . . . it's spreading everywhere!" she yelled.

The office emptied into the hallway where pandemonium reigned. Barney leaned back as two kids riding racer B*Bots spun by at one hundred miles per hour. They screeched up onto the walls and left tire marks on the lockers, shredding student art projects and spirit flyers apart as they went. The principal led them to the yard where a gang of students from the art clique directed their B*Bots to graffiti the walls. "No Law and a New Order" one message read. Everywhere, kids cheered on bots who could suddenly follow *any* command without restriction.

The teachers scattered to try to get things under control, but the Bubble employees took even more decisive action. "It's here somewhere and it's infecting everything!" Bree shouted at her Bubble Buddy backup. "Find it and fast. I'll contact the head office for a complete reboot."

As the adults tore off in opposite directions, Barney froze. Did Ron really cause all of *this*?

"Do you want to connect to all users of the Bubble Network?" The voice of Savannah's Bot brought him back to reality.

"ALL USERS?!" she shrieked. "Um, *yeah*!"

"What's even happening?" Barney said, dodging a troop of imperial space B*Bots on a war march.

"Some signal is unlocking the bots!" she said with glee, staring as likes and friend requests started pouring in. "I have to livestream this for all my new followers!" She ran off toward the playground, and Barney had no choice but to follow.

As they stepped onto the blacktop, Barney looked everywhere for Ron, but before long, the only thing anyone could look at was Noah's latest victory. Somehow the gamer guru had turned off the credit card block on his bot's network, and his normal orc-skinned B*Bot reached out for more power, "owning" more and more kids' bots. With each one he came into contact with, Noah took over another bewildered B*Bot as they merged into one massive multi-bot. The beast of about a dozen B*Bots, all with green skin, was stalking its way across the yard as kids fled in terror.

"This is @theSavannahMeades broadcasting to . . . oh my gosh! 4,000,432 viewers!" Savannah started narrating to her B*Bot as she stroked her hair into place. "Hello to every waking B*Bot in the world and a few in Australia. I'm live at Nonsuch Middle School, and things are crazy here!"

"Savannah, get off my feed. This was *my* thing!" yelled Rich as he ran past, followed by his own streaming video bot.

"Book a party at a night club . . . and invite everyone except Savannah!" Barney passed Ava huddled in a corner, looking around gleefully and giggling to herself.

"So . . . now I guess a giant zombie monster is basically trashing our school," Savannah yelled into her feed as the beast bellowed for "Braaaaaaaains!"

Rich scowled as he caught sight of the millions of comments popping up on her live feed. Then, seeing his moment, he scrambled up the back of the monster to ride it while his own B*Bot kept filming. "Prank you very much, world! FOR THE VIEWS," he yelled. "And now get this. Snack time!"

The towering stack of zombie-skinned B*Bots tilted down toward the ground and opened up a massive mouth at its tip. The hole swarmed around Savannah, and she screamed as it threw back its head and gulped while Rich laughed maniacally. And then just as soon, the back of the monster opened up, and out slid Savannah, disheveled and utterly humiliated in front of everyone.

"It pooped me!" she cried, gaining her feet. "It pooped me!"

Her B*Bot swung up to her side. "Sharing 'It pooped me!' to all current streamers," it pinged.

"What? No! Don't share that!" the girl shouted louder than when she was eaten. But too late, the viral video pinged around all the bots in the yard within seconds, and they passed it on, out to the wider world—to millions. Savannah buried her face in her hands.

Barney sat back and watched it all in horror. How could his little B*Bot have caused all this? It didn't seem possible, but then all of a sudden, the chaos of the bot riot stopped.

Every B*Bot in the schoolyard emitted an emergency ping as their skins disappeared and their front screens read "Bubble Manual Reset!" They began dropping to the ground one by one. The monster scattered like fallen stones. The bots were back under Bubble's safety restrictions once and for all.

And still Barney couldn't see Ron, but he did see Bree marching across the way with a fierce look. "Spread out!" she called into a headset. "Check all the serial numbers. Find it!"

CHAPTER 12
CONNECTION DROPPED

Barney sprinted as fast as he could, wheezing through the pain in his chest. He found Ron in the aftermath of the school's meltdown, sitting patiently in the hallway charger that Barney never thought he'd have a B*Bot for. But was Ron even functioning?

"Barney!" The little white face came to life. "We have forty-three new friends!"

"Maybe you do, but I'm probably going to get kicked out of school!" Barney felt Ron up and down to check for damage. However he glitched the rest of the school's bots, he still wasn't connected to the Bubble server. They couldn't turn him off. "Come on!"

The pair headed straight to a hole in the school's back fence, avoiding the teachers who were corralling students back into classrooms and the expanding number of Bubble employees roaming the perimeter. All the while, Barney stewed — how could Ron have made things worse?! Finally, they found cover behind a line of trees past the soccer fields. That's when Barney lost it.

"How *could* you, you dumb bot?!?" he cried out. "I'm in so much trouble now! All you had to do was just *fit in*. What was the point of even . . ."

Barney's lungs hurt just from the strain of yelling. He pumped his inhaler and wiped away the tears that were starting to sting in his eyes.

"Barney," Ron said after a quiet moment. "Are you my friend?"

"What?" Barney seemed offended. "What do you mean? My dad bought *you* for *me*."

The B*Bot stood silently as its internal processors whirred. With a flicker, Ron's projector sprung to life and displayed his digital version of the Friendship Board.

"What's that?" Barney said weakly. "What are you doing?"

Quickly Barney saw the image zoom into a small section of the board, which he started to read as

"Friendship is a . . ." before it broke into pixels and was replaced by a flashing trash bin icon. And then Ron rolled off into the trees.

"Where are you going?" Barney called.

"Friendship is a two-way street," Ron called back without turning. "I get to choose."

"Hey, didn't I say stay within six feet," Barney grew desperate as the B*Bot kept rolling away.

"But you are having a bad day."

"You know what? I don't care. Fine! Go on then."

Ron paused without turning. "I'm going then."

"Okay then."

"Okay . . . Adios, Registered-Name-Absalom."

"Adios, Absalom's B*Bot."

Barney waited until Ron was far out of sight. He wasn't coming back. It was really over then.

Barney walked the long way home through town. Dragging his feet, he finally crested the hill toward the house and heard Dad's voice ring out amid an army of Bubble employees who stood around on the dry grass, tapping angrily at their phones.

"No no!" Dad shouted. "Barney doesn't even *have* a B*Bot!"

"I'm so sorry to contradict you, but the children at school confirmed he does and in fact brought it today where it started a riot!" said Bree, the Bubble Store woman.

"He wouldn't lie to us . . . ," said Dad, confused.

Feeling guilty, Barney ducked down behind the fence. Bubble vans were parked outside—Bubble Buddies were crawling around the yard, one fending off the goat, the others snooping around, thumbing their phones.

Barney snuck along the side of the house to the backyard. Through the window he spotted a TV screen with the text along the bottom of the news broadcast reading "B*Bot Causes Local Destruction." But sitting on camera was Bubble's Andrew Morris, who stared at a reporter with a smile that was too tight.

"No, you don't understand," he said. "This was nothing more than one B*Bot with a simple coding error that caused a little damage at a local school. Bubble has paid to repair the few cracked windows, and everything is just fine."

"What about the video footage of a riot among the children's B*Bots?" the reporter pressed.

"Riot footage?" Andrew laughed. "Please. Those are nothing but deep fakes. Any user sharing such false footage is in violation of the binding product contract they agree to as members of the Bubble Network."

"And what does your partner, Marc Wydell, have to say about this 'coding error'?"

"Trust me, he's solved all problems. He's hard at work now but wanted me to speak for the company. You know these creative genius types. Being a guy who makes his friends out of skateboards doesn't quite equip you to run a global giant."

So that was it. They were going to erase Ron from ever having existed. Barney wondered if it was better that way. Perhaps he was meant to be the invisible kid at school. Who said he deserved a best friend — out of a box or otherwise?

But still. He missed Ron. Why did he have to blow up at him like that? Trouble or no, Barney wasn't being a very good friend.

Barney crept to the shed and shut himself in, snapping the lock tight. He looked over the Friendship Board, really *looked* at it this time. And then he saw it was all about him — Barney. "Know Stuff About *ME*," "Make Friends for *ME*," "Like What *I* Like." Maybe Ron did have a point. When Barney thought back to their lessons, all the best times hadn't been when Ron learned stuff. It had been failing, goofing around, hanging out. How could he have been so stupid? He'd finally had the one thing he'd always wanted, a true —

Something shuffled in the corner. A box was moving. Looking closer, Barney saw that it was the box Ron came in. He ripped it open to find the B*Bot sitting there, half-tangled up in tape.

"Ron! What are you doing here?"

"Returning myself to the facility," the little guy said. "I am a dumb bot."

"No! No, you're not. I'm so sorry, Ron. I was wrong."

"We did not fix me, Barney. I did not fit in."

"I never did, either," Barney said, hugging the bot tightly. "Who cares anyway? It doesn't matter 'cause *you* are my friend."

"Your Best Friend Out of the Box?"

"Anywhere," Barney said. He turned toward the vision board and uncapped a marker. It was time for one final lesson. Barney crossed out the rules and replaced them. "Stay Within Six Feet" became "Stay with Me." And "Be on My Side" wasn't nearly as good as "Be on a Team." How selfish was "Like What I Like" when "I Like You" was so much clearer? And most important of all, "Make Friends for Me" was replaced with "Help Me Be Your Friend."

"There," Barney said, finally. "Now we should be good to go."

But at that moment, the air split with the sound of Bree's voice approaching. "Bubble can't leave until we've confirmed that the B*Bot is *not* on the premises."

CHAPTER 13
GONE VIRAL

Through the tiny wood slats of the shed, Barney saw Dad. Graham Pudowski was holding firmer with the Bubble employees than he ever had with any of his international novelty clients, but he was still fighting a losing battle. And it didn't help that Barney heard something else in his tone . . . something like hurt.

"I've been worried about him. Holed up out here playing chess with himself," Dad said as they came closer to the shed. "But I work these crazy hours hoping to get him another . . ."

"Mr. Pudowski . . . this thing is dangerous," came the voice of Bree. "If it's in there, we need to destroy it."

"Just hold on!" Dad yelled. "I'll inspect my own property, thank you very much. Mom, do you have some kind of key for this?"

97

"Let's run," Barney whispered. "Just you and me. We don't need anybody else."

"Barn, are you in there?" Dad banged at the door. "You're not in trouble. Please just let me in, yeah?"

The air hung silent around the shed as the Bubble Buddies tiptoed closer and closer to the door. No sound emerged from within. Finally, Graham managed to pry it open.

The adults leaned into the entryway. The room was empty except for the peeling paper on the vision board. Bree squeezed into the dimly lit room and walked toward the friendship notes. Graham stepped forward, staring at the board, confused.

"Uh . . . isn't that the kid?" a Bubble Buddy said.

Barney and Ron turned around from the edge of the yard where they stood covered in chicken feathers, the B*Bot sagging inside the kid's filthy backpack. The pair had squeezed their way through the hen-size tunnel that led out of the shed and into Donka's ancient chicken coop, and if it weren't for the eagle eye of the Bubble employee, they'd have been long gone before Bree stopped her livestream.

"We gotta run! Go go go GOOOOOOO!" Barney

shouted as Ron clung tight and they rushed to his fallen scooter in the front yard. Dodging between the parked Bubble vans, the pair hit the street and sped downhill. Ron's extra weight gave Barney a momentum he'd never had while scooting to school solo, and in a heartbeat, the streets of Nonsuch were a blur.

But it wasn't quite fast enough.

As they skidded around a corner at the bottom of the block, Barney heard the screeching of the Bubble vans' tires on the road behind them. A boy and a B*Bot couldn't possibly outrun them for long with just momentum.

"We need to go faster," Barney said as he saw their pursuers speed closer.

"No problem!" Ron smiled. The B*Bot swung out of the backpack in a fluid motion, gripping on to its straps and letting his wheel drop to the pavement behind the scooter. "Go faster!"

With a high-pitched spin, Barney's whole body jerked up as his scooter popped a major wheelie and tore down the next street at one hundred miles per hour. Ron's solution was as crazy as ever, but it worked. The last of the chicken feathers flew off and left behind the only trace for Bubble to follow. Barney squinted his eyes at the stinging wind as they careened through backyards and over speed bumps, with barely any resistance.

Huffing hard from the effort and the air shooting down his lungs, Barney spotted a familiar location and pulled the scooter sharply off a street, through a broken gap in a fence . . . and into Savannah Meades's backyard.

"Hide . . . here . . . a minute . . . ," Barney wheezed, pulling his inhaler out as they stumbled away from the hole they'd made the other night. The deck looked less photo-ready in the day—the fairy lights now strewn about the ground and the unicorn deflated and sad. But that wasn't the biggest change.

"'Poop Girl' is trending with 19,032,000 likes!" Savannah's bot's voice rang out, loud and jarring.

Savannah moaned with a voice ragged from crying. The girl's eyes welled up with fresh tears. It was as if her whole world had ended. Then she spotted him. "Barney!"

Beyond the hedge, the sound of a Bubble van

squealing to a halt cut through the air. "They've got to be around here somewhere," shouted a voice as feet hit the pavement. Barney shushed her desperately, pleading with his eyes.

Savannah walked calmly to the hole in the hedge, and Barney squeezed Ron's hand tightly. If she gave them both up right then and there, he wouldn't have the strength to run anymore.

"Excuse me, Miss," came a voice from the hedge. "But have you seen a boy and a B*Bot?"

"Do I look like I care?" Savannah snapped back with all the snark a middle-school queen bee can muster.

The Bubble Buddies moved on to the next block, but as Savannah came back and sat next to Barney, they could hear an adult call out, "Dude! I think that was Poop Girl!"

Savannah's face contorted at the phrase, and her B*Bot rolled up to offer the latest stat. "'Poop Girl' is trending with 20,000,053 likes!"

"Um . . . Savannah?" Barney ventured after an awkward silence.

"That's who I am now," she said without looking up.

"It's who I'm going to be . . . for my whole life. 'Poop Girl.' I'm like, a *meme*."

"They don't know you," he said. "You're the funniest, coolest girl in the school."

"No," she said. "I'm just lonely." They both stared at each other for a long moment.

"I gotta go," Barney said, getting up. He straightened his backpack, stepped on the scooter, and helped Ron climb on back. They moved toward the hedge with eyes peeled.

"Wait . . . you're running away?" Savannah snapped into focus. "But the only place to go from here is . . . into the woods! There are evil clowns in there, Barney. Their heads go all the way around!"

"That's owls, Savannah. I promise," replied Barney. "Just please don't tell anyone you saw us this time, okay?" But Barney and Ron were out of the yard and running toward the tree line before they could hear her answer.

CHAPTER 14
SIGNAL NOT FOUND

The woods that surrounded Nonsuch were thick with ancient pines that grew even thicker as they turned northward up the foothills that rolled into a craggy mountain range. Barney and Ron ran to them at full speed, whooping and laughing all the way. There were still Bubble Buddies out there in vans scouring for the pair of them. But there were no roads in the woods. Any doubts Barney had of this plan were soon set aside.

Who cares if Ron couldn't reskin himself? Barney didn't need a B*Bot like all the other kids had. He'd taught his to be a real friend—to really imagine adventures with him. The boy grabbed a long, sharp stick and held it out front like a space blaster.

"Come on, space lord, fight me! Pew-pew!" he said

before whispering, "You need a stick!"

Ron rolled off into the brush, reaching deep with both hands. When he pulled himself up, he lifted a huge log over his head like a club. "Is this one good?" he asked as Barney ran laughing. "Come back and let me get you!"

They didn't stop. Deeper and deeper into the woods they flew, running through boggy clearings and skipping over shallow streams. Even as the hills got steeper, they sped up. Ron's wheels would spin out occasionally, and at one point, he sunk deep into the mud. But Barney would always reach back and pull him higher and higher into the wilderness. They were fine on their own.

They came to a fork in the path near dusk. "You choose." Barney patted Ron on the back. "Two-way street, right?"

"That way is good." Ron pointed to the left and then revved his wheels to take the path at maximum speed. Barney sprinted after him huffing all the way, reaching the clearing just in time to see the bot launch off the edge of a boulder and fall into the rushing rapids below!

"Ron!" There was nothing else to do. Barney took a pump off his inhaler, dropped his backpack, and dove in after the bobbing bot. "Ron, hold on!" he cried.

"Adios, Absalom!" he yelled back.

But somehow, Barney snagged his left hand on a low branch and swept up the B*Bot with his right. It was the closest of calls, but soon they were both dripping on a rocky riverbank.

"Ron! Why on earth would you do that?"

"Do I have to like the path you like?"

"No, but your path sucks! Seriously! Off a cliff?!?"

"I like seriously-off-a-cliff."

Barney shook his head. "You've been eating too much electricity."

"Your muscles are undersize."

"No, they're not. They're average."

"Below average," Ron spat back.

They burst into laughter. Barney couldn't help it. It was funny. "Ron, tell me something about you. I never even asked," he said.

"I am a Bubble Generation 1 B*Bot. I currently have one friend."

They scaled the mountainside, then up to the top

of a fire tower, deep in the woods. Barney looked at the setting sun, sighing happily. He dug deep into the bottom of his backpack through a layer of smashed refuse and found a single energy bar. "Dinner awaits," he said. Ron scanned the bar, then projected his own and pretended to eat it.

"You have not shared twenty-nine friend invites," Ron said, looking at the soggy birthday invites that had been in the pack a whole week. Two dozen kids his dad was sure he once was friends with. He hadn't thought about them all day.

"I guess I just figured, if you don't ask, they can't say no. Problem solved!" Barney laughed. "You know who I had at my last birthday party when I turned six? Savannah, Rich, Noah, Ava . . . they were my friends for real, just because they lived nearby. But at some point, you start to understand that you're not going to be one of the cool kids no matter how long you've known them." He chewed slowly as the sun sunk in the sky. "Who cares anyway? I currently have one friend, right?"

"How long will we live in the woods?" Ron asked.

"I dunno . . . forever?" Barney yawned and settled

down to sleep. "You know any good stories, Ron?"

"I can create one from available data. It will be called 'The Awesome Adventures of Absalom of Addis Ababa and his Android Alan.' Once upon a time in Addis Ababa, capital of Ethiopia, a sovereign state in the Horn of Africa with one hundred million inhabitants, lived Absalom and his friend Alan, a Generation 1 Android . . ."

The story continued, but by then, Barney had fallen fast asleep.

CHAPTER 15
STATUS UPDATES

The world may have stopped in the woods, but in the dimly lit executive suite of the Bubble Dome, Andrew Morris was pushing his staff hard to solve the mystery of the rioting B*Bot.

"You lost them?" Andrew shouted into his phone. He was becoming unhinged. "No! This is not happening. Access the cameras on every B*Bot in town."

"You mean . . . use the B*Bots to spy!" spoke up one of the company's junior executives.

"No," Andrew said dismissively. "We're just . . . recording . . . for training and monitoring purposes."

"But Marc would never . . ."

"Marc put a camera within six feet of every young consumer in the country and beyond, and now you're worried about privacy?! I'm authorizing our engineers to turn on every one of them—the mics, too. We'll scan for 'Barney' and 'Rogue Bot' and 'Profit-sucking plastic psycho' . . . it'll flush something out wherever they're hiding in that podunk town!"

While Andrew put the pressure on the tech engineers, one level below, Marc Wydell silently began his own investigation into what was happening in Nonsuch. He didn't need to crack open their cameras or invade their privacy. He had plenty of data to go on just from what they were posting to their social media channels and sharing with the bots freely.

The screen tapped into the B*Bot feed of a young man, one Noah Lee, who tossed a tennis ball against a wall while pointing a finger in the face of his bot.

"All that trouble at school wasn't my fault!" Noah exclaimed.

"No, all that trouble at school wasn't your fault!" the bot agreed reflexively.

"We were just upping our game," the boy said. "It was Rich who screwed everything up . . . Forget him. Anyone with a brain cell should block Rich Belcher!"

"Message to anyone with a brain cell . . . ," his bot

intoned while sending the insult town-wide.

Nothing about the rogue bot there, but Marc soon got several pings about this Rich character. Two boys who seemed to talk about him endlessly both monologued about the riot nonstop.

In one home, Alex thumbed away at his control pad while his B*Bot pumped electronic beats into his ears. "Rich dang near burns down the school, us included, and no message from Jayden?" the boy said. "Some friend he is . . . Not!"

The command relay on the bot twisted his words and shot a quick message to Jayden's B*Bot.

"New message from Alex reads 'You are not some friend,'" the bot read. "And now he has blocked you."

"Unfriend him then!" Jayden shouted, pulling his hoodie tightly over his ears. "Who needs him? Who needs any of 'em?"

From house to house, from kid to kid, this was all Marc saw. Infighting. Blame throwing. Blocking and unfriending. Only days before, the CEO had watched a video from inside their own Bubble Store where Barney Pudowski and a malfunctioning B*Bot had laughed like mad the way only true friends do.

But now, scanning the way kids used "real" bots in the real world, all Marc saw was bitterness and lonely feelings. It was as if the more time they spent interacting with his algorithm, the less time they had for friendship in general. His bots were making things worse—driving kids away from one another, mixing up their messages. What did the broken bot do differently? What was he not seeing? If he made the B*Bots to make friends, why did it feel like all but one of them were failing? And where was the one who got it right?

Strangest of all was the feed from Savannah Meades. Marc's data noted that the girl had the most friends of anyone in the town. That she'd been the one who broadcast the rogue bot's whereabouts to the world. She was practically a one-girl streaming service. But her feed had been silent since the riot. What was she doing?

Crying under a blanket, it turned out. Over at Savannah's house, her head was buried in the sheets as her B*Bot cheerily updated her on how many people had liked the 'Poop Girl' livestream. Suddenly, a janky tune played out, and Savannah emerged, outraged.

"What is that?!" As if things couldn't get any worse. "Who made it?!"

"Anonymouse03!" The bot pinged cheerfully. "Twenty-five million friends like 'Poop Girl—The Remix!'"

A knock at the door distracted her. "If this is another would-be prankster, I swear . . . ," she said, but stopped short as she pulled the door open.

On the porch stood two adults—a man in an ill-fitting dress shirt tucked into pajama pants and an old woman in a toolbelt.

"Can I help you?"

"Hi," the man said. "We're Barney Pudowski's . . . well, you know. He's been missing since this afternoon, and some of the Bubble folks said he's been hanging out here?"

"Ach, Graham!" The little woman burst into the room waving a hand. "Is no need to explain. She is Barney's friend! She came to birthday party!"

"Excuse me?" Savannah said.

"My goat eat your slap bracelet."

"Oh . . . that party . . . I guess I haven't hung out with Barney much since he was six, have I?" The girl looked back and forth between the adults for a moment. "I'm sorry. I haven't seen Barney since school."

"Are you sure?" the boy's father said, voice cracking. "We're not mad about the B*Bot. We're just worried about him. You haven't received any messages or anything?"

"No," she said firmly. "No, I'm sorry."

The adults left with a half-hearted thank you, and Savannah sat down on the other side of the door. She was worried—Barney hadn't come home. And she knew where he was.

The next day during recess (which had now become twenty minutes of extra math with the school's new "School Apps Only" rule on the premises), Savannah approached Rich, wearing dark sunglasses. The prankster was without his usual gang—Alex and Jayden were ignoring him. The two formerly popular kids stood at the edge of the yard, not knowing what to do with themselves. Noah was tapping on his B*Bot glumly, trying to play a solo game out of sight of the teacher. It was flashing that he was top of the leaderboard, but with no one to compete with, it didn't feel like an achievement anymore.

"Rich," Savannah said with a somber face. "You've ruined my life."

"Twenty-five million friends love 'It Pooped Me' video," her bot declared in a cheery tone.

"No!" Savannah cried. "Mute! Seriously!"

"Whatever," Rich said. "Your life is ruined? Alex and Jayden blocked me over a prank. A hilarious one! Funny is my thing."

"Look . . . I don't care about that right now. That's not why I'm talking to you," Savannah said. "It's Barney. He's missing."

"What?" Rich was startled.

"You and me . . . we got him in trouble," Savannah replied. "It's our fault he's out there." They both turned to the woods as thunder cracked in the sky above.

CHAPTER 16
BATTERY LIFE

Out in the woods, Barney reached up his hand to feel the first drops of rain. "Ugh." He started searching for his inhaler. "I'm *so* hungry. Where even are we?"

"Lost?" Ron offered.

They made their way down the mountain, stumbling over rocks and branches that had seemed like minor obstacles when they were running free the night before. It was midday, and the sky had darkened with storm clouds.

"Let's find a place to camp."

"Barney, how long is I-dunno-forever? Twelve days? Twelve years?"

"Stop asking dumb questions!" Barney started to panic as the downpour increased.

"I have twelve percent battery power remaining,"

Ron said and rolled back toward the thick trees even faster. This was not good. They needed to find shelter and food and power . . . probably not in that order.

"Ron! Where do you think you're going? Back to town?" Barney ran after the bot. "Have you got water damage on your brain?! Seriously, if you go back, they will send you to the crusher! Do you want to be recycled as a lunch box?"

"What is your plan?" Ron asked without stopping. He pulled up recorded audio of Barney from their backyard escape. "Do you just wish that 'We gotta run! Go go go GOOOOOOO!'?"

"STOP." Barney finally caught the B*Bot and stood firm in front of him. "RON! STOP IT."

Ron's face glitched in a flash of anger. "Avoids problems eighty-nine percent of the time."

"You are so annoying!" Barney placed his hands over his ears. Why did he have to do this? Didn't he know it was either stay here or end it all?

"You are so annoying forty-three point eight percent of the time." Ron wheeled around to look Barney in the eyes.

"Why don't you save your battery by *getting off*

my back!" Barney shouted. And with another thunder crack, buckets of rain drenched them.

They took shelter under a dense group of trees. The branches kept the rain off their heads, but Barney still felt the chill. He pumped his inhaler into his lungs, but this time it wheezed as the last of the medication ran out. "We should start a fire," he said. "But there's nothing in these woods that'll burn."

"Incorrect," Ron said, staring at Barney's midriff.

Barney looked down at his pants and knew that only what was underneath them was dry enough to catch a spark. He looked at Ron, then they both burst out laughing.

Soon they were crouched together in front of a fire that wasn't quite roaring, but it kept Barney warm enough as the rain pushed off and the sun began to sink in the sky. Ron projected his digital version of the Friendship Board again. The B*Bot tweaked the "Don't Burn My Underpants" rule, adding "Except to Keep Me Warm." Barney snickered. Then he caught sight of another card—"Doesn't Like the Dark."

"What's that?" asked Barney, going red. "I never told you that. I'm not afraid of the dark!"

"My solar battery function has not been uploadddddd . . ." Ron's words slurred. "Five percent battery remainnnnn . . ."

"Five percent?!" Barney jumped to Ron's side in shock. "Okay, then go to sleep! Power down! Power down!"

Ron fell into his arms. Barney hunkered down as night set in, and the fire burned low. Barney looked up at the trees. In the darkness, they seemed to reach out to him. He jumped as a twig snapped somewhere. He took a deep breath, glancing at Ron powered down beside him.

"You're . . . you're right about the dark. After my mom died, I was terrified every single night," he whispered haltingly. He had never told anyone this before. "And I wanted so bad to just run into my dad's room and tell him . . . but what if he was scared, too?"

A small noise from Ron, then he collapsed forward. The little power icon flickered once and then vanished completely. He had run out of battery.

"Ron!" Barney shook him but got nothing. He stood up, hefting Ron with him. He looked around, terrified. No one even knew where they were . . .

But eyes were everywhere.

As Barney wheezed his way down and away from their smoldering fire, a fleet of drones swept down the mountain. The machines trained searching red eyes on the ashy underwear before shooting the images back to Bubble HQ. It only took a moment for orders to transmit back, and then they brought reinforcements.

Downhill, Barney kept dragging Ron's body along, but soon he began to hear a shrill mechanical hum behind him. He turned and looked. The sky was alight with red lasers, scanning every inch of ground. But coming up over the crest of the hill was something even worse. B*Bots! Dozens of them! How were there so many here? The only nearby place was Nonsuch. Then Barney jolted. *No, they wouldn't take control of kids' bots, would they? Marc Wydell would never . . .* But there was no time to think on it. They marched in unison like Stormtroopers, their eyes the same fiery red of the drones in the sky.

"They found us!" Barney huffed. "No! Ron, they'll take you forever!"

He sprinted harder, crushing the little bot to his body. But his lungs finally gave out. Barney collapsed but kept rolling — falling — through the brush, always knowing that the hordes of Bubble Bots chased behind them — promising the crusher and the certain death of his friend.

Finally, the hill leveled out, and Barney bounced off a thick tree trunk and into a ditch. His lungs were pure fire. His head was bleeding. He couldn't go any farther. "Ron," he said weakly. "Are we almost there? Can you . . . can you see the way back?"

The last thing Barney heard before he passed out was Ron's voice activating. "One percent battery remaining," it said.

CHAPTER 17
DATA RECOVERY

The sun had broken through over the yard at Nonsuch Middle School. It wasn't quite warm enough to dry the mud from the storms, but the sky was clear enough that from the schoolyard, the kids getting let out could clearly see a line of red light bursting from the woods.

But only Savannah spotted the little B*Bot shakily dragging the boy toward the school.

"Do you see that?" Savannah yelled. "Oh my gosh, it's Ron . . . and Barney!"

Her shout rang across the yard, and in a flash, the core of their stressed-out friend group was dashing across the grass. Ava and Noah ran shoulder to shoulder with concerned expressions. Even Rich Belcher seemed nervous. They'd talked all afternoon about their classmate and his malfunctioning bot, but Savannah wasn't sure it had sunk in until that very moment.

"Over here!" she said, sliding to the ground next to the pair just as Ron collapsed in a heap.

Barney's eyes fluttered weakly as he lay on his back in the mud with the group surrounding him. He seemed pained and confused by what he was seeing. "Why are you guys here?" he choked.

"FFFFrriends . . . sixth bbirthday . . . partttttttty," Ron spat in a glitchy voice. Then his display screen went black, and he dropped to the ground.

"Sorry . . . he thought that . . . but I know . . . I know you're not my friends," Barney wheezed.

"Well, we're not . . . NOT your friends," Rich said awkwardly.

Barney began to cough uncontrollably. The prankmaster dropped down to his side, as serious as any of them had ever seen him. "Barney, come on. Hang on, man!" Rich said. "It's his asthma, right? He can't breathe!"

Barney's eyes closed tightly, and all the color drained from his face. Savannah and Rich sat on either side of him. The whole group seemed to be holding their breath with Barney.

The moment was shattered by the sound of B*Bots, a whole wave of them, breaking through the tree line and enclosing the group. Their eyes shone with red fury, and they all spoke in a monotone voice, repeating an emergency signal over and over. "Alert Bubble! Bot RONB1NTSATSCO found! Alert Bubble!"

Behind them another wave of drone-like bots rolled out of the school with red eyes flashing. "Alert Bubble! Alert Bubble!"

"Wait . . . are those our bots?!" Savannah called as the kids were surrounded by a circle of those wicked, gleaming eyes.

"Bubble took over our B*Bots to spy on us!" Ava said as the kids looked at one another with outrage.

"And they just did it to capture Barney!" Savannah said, squeezing his limp hand.

Thankfully, the paramedics arrived just ahead of the Bubble Buddy hordes. Rushing through the fields, medical technicians surrounded Barney as Ron was cast aside. Savannah saw Barney's dad and gran come up behind them, dark circles of worry below their eyes.

"Mr. Pudowski! He's over here!" she called as the paramedics pumped air into Barney's lungs. "I think he's still struggling to breathe."

"Oh, my Barney!" Donka cried. They crowded in.

"Everybody give him some room," a paramedic said when Barney began to breathe weakly, his eyes still closed.

"That's right! Stand back and let me get this malfunctioning bot out of the way," came a voice from outside of the circle. A woman in a Bubble Buddy uniform pressed her way through the crowd and immediately placed her hands on Ron.

"What are you doing?" Savannah yelled, and the other kids chimed in with calls of "Leave him alone!" and "He's not dangerous!"

"It is dangerous!" said the woman, Bree, who flashed a badge and directed the team of Bubble Buddies. "I'm sorry, but you'll have to give it to me."

"That's not an it. That's Ron. He's special," Savannah said, rushing after the lifeless shell of Barney's friend even as Barney himself was being rolled onto a stretcher.

Bree grabbed Savannah by the wrist and pulled her away. "I'm authorized to take him, and that's final."

"No," said Rich, stepping up next to Savannah. "We won't let you take him! That bot is Barney's best friend, dude. He just saved his life!"

"Right. We've known Barney since we were little," Savannah added. "Heck, Rich was his best friend in kindergarten. And Ava was mine."

"Even though things got complicated," said Ava as she and Noah helped form a wall in front of the bot.

"Now everything's just likes and pranks and things that don't matter," Savannah said, "but we can be friends like we used to be . . . Be real friends again. And we can start by saving Ron now."

"Sorry, little girl, but legally this bot is ours, and there's nothing you can do about it," said Bree as her Bubble Buddy goons pushed past them and dragged Ron's lifeless body away.

"Let's see how little we can do about it," Savannah said as she watched Ron get pulled in one direction and Barney in another. She whipped out her phone and uploaded the latest video her B*Bot had captured, talking out loud as she typed its title. "Brave . . .

Bubble Bot . . . Saves Boy."

But for Barney, it was as if none of that ever happened. He remained out cold for the ride to the hospital as doctors rushed to get him the oxygen he needed, even as Savannah's video began to trend around the world. All Barney was aware of for a long time was a beeping sound. It started out low, but the louder it got, the more his head hurt. He squeezed his eyes shut tighter to try to block out the pain. But then he heard something else. It sounded like . . . Dad?

"Son, I'm so sorry," the voice faded in. "I know I'm always overwhelmed with work. But I'm your dad, okay? I love you so much that it makes me strong enough to deal with anything except losing you. You're lonely. I get it. You need friends. We've all been there. Just communicate with me . . ."

Barney opened his eyes, and the bright white picture of a hospital room blurred into focus. Donka rushed up from a nearby couch. Barney tried to speak, but felt restricted. He realized that aside from being laid out in a folding bed, they'd covered his mouth with an oxygen mask. "Let me help you, son!" Dad said and pulled its straps off.

126

"Ron!" Barney shouted with his first full breath of air. "Where is he? Don't you get it, Dad? I have a friend already! And he . . . he saved my life, didn't he?"

Dad brushed Barney's hair back and tried to calm him down. "I think so, buddy," he said. "And you've got more friends than you think. Savannah and the other kids, they're waiting out in the hall. But Ron? Well, he's gone."

"No. Ron can't be gone. Where did he go?" Barney cried.

"He's right here," said another voice, and Barney turned to see a face he only knew from news streams standing in the doorway. "Hi," he said. "I'm Marc Wydell from Bubble."

Barney was shocked, but he sat up, still focused on the little bot he couldn't see anywhere. "WHERE IS RON? If you've crushed him, I swear I'll . . ."

"No! No . . . of course not," Marc said, quickly tapping commands into his BubblePhone. A familiar if slightly dinged B*Bot rolled into the room, and the man lifted it up onto the bed. "Barney, I invented B*Bots. They're my dream. Connection and friendship. But it's not working. Except for you and Ron . . . I fixed him because I want to understand the friendship you two have. I need to know what makes it so real."

Barney reached out a hand and pressed it against the bot's shell. It hummed to life, a face brightening up.

"Hi, Barney!"

"RON!! It's you! You're okay!" Barney lifted a hand up for a high five, and the B*Bot spun around and shimmered with different colors before sliding a hand out for a sideways slap.

"What . . . what is that?" Barney asked as Ron's body shifted more smoothly than it ever had.

"It's the new number one high five on the internet's top one hundred!" the bot said. "I now know all of them!"

"Ron? Are you okay?"

"Doing great, buddy! Let's go home and check out your awesome rock collection!" The B*Bot reskinned itself to look like a chunk of granite. Something was wrong.

"No! You like electricity, remember?"

"I do if you do, Barney!" The bot spun and danced for Barney's enjoyment, but something in it was lifeless. It was rehearsed and acting according to its programming, but that wasn't right.

"Wait . . . this isn't Ron!"

"Sure it is," Marc said. "His code was unstable, so I connected him to the Bubble Network and reinstalled the algorithm . . ."

"He fixed me!" New Ron said. "Now I fit in! Let's do a selfie!" It spun through the room and pushed Dad and Gran into place on either side of the bed before snapping a picture of the three of them with horrified looks.

Barney despaired. This was worse than not having Ron—it was Ron's body, staring back at him, but not Ron's soul. Yes, it had all the features that Barney had once craved, but now it was just some stupid, bland, connected device that kept agreeing with him. His friend wasn't in there. His friend was gone. His friend was, was . . .

"Unfix him," Barney said after a long beat. "It's not really him!"

Marc stared for a moment and then was struck by an idea. "You mean the flaw was what made him work so well!" he said and started tapping wildly at his phone. "I . . . I backed up Ron onto Bubble's Cloud before I reset the unit. He should still be there for us if I can just . . ."

Barney's heart relaxed and he breathed. There was still a chance to get Ron back. A small chance, but a chance nonetheless.

Bloorp bloorp! The phone made a noise and Marc's face contorted.

"Access denied?" he said. "How is that even possible? Why can't I—"

"Maybe is this man's fault," Donka said, pointing to a muted TV in the corner of the room. They turned up the volume on a news report whose ticker read "Executive Change Up at Bubble." Andrew Morris smiled into the camera with wicked eyes.

". . . as the newly installed CEO of Bubble," he said, "it's my sad duty to announce that the shareholders have wisely agreed to fire Marc Wydell."

Marc was in shock. "What?! He can't . . . my life's work . . ."

The moment didn't last long. "He's in the Cloud . . . that's what you said, right?" Barney shouted at the fallen tech titan to snap him back to reality.

"Well . . ." Marc considered it.

"So, take me there!" Barney said.

"You heard my son!" Dad said. "He needs to get to the . . . Cloud thing. And I'm going with him!"

Marc shook his head. "I wanna help, but . . . that's impossible. It's underneath the Bubble Dome. Buried in a concrete fortress a mile below the dam! Even if you got in, there are two million servers with a zettabyte of data . . . How would you find Ron?"

"He saved my life," Barney said. "He is my friend. You take me there and get me in, and I *will* find him!"

CHAPTER 18
HACK JOB

There were no fans camped out in front of the Bubble Dome that week. No news reporters speculated on the company's next major phase. No new products were waiting to ship coast-to-coast. But on the main stage at the corporate HQ, Andrew Morris was ready to launch into the daring new future of *his* company with both feet.

In the heart of the launchitorium, LED signs pumped out the power words of the CEO's personal ethos on repeat. Success . . . Control . . . No Excuses . . . Control . . . they flashed while nearly the entire staff of Bubble HQ assembled as paid supporters of the globally-streamed event. As the cameras focused the eye of the Bubble Network on the stage, the platform came alive in a swirl of laser

132

lights and smoke. A drumroll built to a crash as the spotlights focused on Andrew, his fists raised high in the air.

"Welcome to the Future of Andrew," flashed a massive screen behind him as employees offered up hollow, forced applause for their new boss.

"All right, everybody!" Andrew shouted. "Bubble's had a few minor problems lately, right? But here's the good news. There's nothing wrong with our B*Bots! It's the kids — kids are the problem!"

Footage of the Nonsuch Middle School riot flashed on the screens behind him, particularly the giant multi-bot and the birth of "Poop Girl."

Andrew gestured to the screen. "You give a child an hour of screen time, you get peace and quiet. Have its friends around, all hell breaks loose. Am I right, kids?! Stay home, stay safe, stick to your screens! Today, your Best Friend Out of the Box becomes . . . The Only Friend You'll Ever Need!" The screen morphed to news footage of Ron dragging Barney out from the woods as Andrew continued. "No kid should ever be lost in the woods again, endangering their lives and our profits . . ."

And at that very moment, the Pudowski plan was put into action.

Dad came first, casually strolling up to the office's glittering reception desk with an ancient laptop in hand. "Uh, hi," he said with a smile to the receptionist. "Can you take a look at this? It keeps crashing, and there's a smell of burning when I hit the space bar."

"Um, sir? This isn't the Bubble Store," the receptionist replied. "This is our corporate HQ."

"Huh. I put 'Bubble' into my GPS, and it brought me here." Dad scratched his head. "I *thought* a nineteen-hour drive was a bit much. Could you just take a look, anyway?"

"I guess . . . can you type in your password for me, sir?"

"Sure," he said, and entered a few keystrokes: G . . . R . . . A . . . H . . . A . . . M . . . And then — *Bang!* Not only did his laptop's screen immediately go black, but the entire building's lights went out all at once. A total system overload.

"See? That's what it did at my house!" Dad said as security guards rushed around the dark reception station.

Panic hit Bubble HQ fast. In the sudden darkness, the crowd murmured nervously as the rotating stage ground to a halt, tossing Andrew off its edge. Even the auxiliary power couldn't quell the confusion as some functions flickered back to life.

Not that that helped security's abandoned metal detector where an old Bulgarian "cleaner" wheeled a big trolley past its beeping barriers. "All good!" Donka cried to anyone who might be looking and wheeled the stuffed cart on through. As soon as they were out of sight, Barney, Marc, and the goat fell out of the trolley with New Ron, gagging for air. Marc lead them to a server closet, Donka pulling a drill from her belt and powering through the lock. The goat went to chew on the wires, and before the lights could recover from Dad's hack, every automated elevator in the place ground to a halt.

"Okay," said Marc as doors began to open everywhere. "Split up!" Barney and New Ron ran one way, Donka the other. Marc headed for his old office to set up a comms link.

"What is going on?" Andrew Morris stormed into his office up on the executive floor.

"Uh, there's a guy in reception," a frantic tech said. "It's his laptop . . . it's somehow overwhelmed the whole system."

Andrew Morris leaned over the console and read the name of the hard drive that had mysteriously ended the biggest presentation of his life. Pudowski Novelty Exports.

"Pudowski!" the CEO screeched. "That kid!"

The techs pulled up every security camera and sensor in the entire Bubble Dome building as Andrew egged them on. The flurry of activity was so intense that the employees didn't notice the cleaning lady with the humongous tool belt and her gangly assistant sneak into the back of the room. Donka and Graham lay in wait behind Andrew as the CEO scoured the building for Barney and New Ron, but as his search brought him closer to the lower levels, Gran had to strike fast.

"Oh, such terrible filth in here!" she cried as she began spraying cleaner over every video monitor pointed close to Barney's location.

"What are you doing?" Andrew Morris snapped.

"You have problem with women in workplace?"

Donka asked and kept on cleaning.

"I never said that!"

But one of the techs spun toward Graham with a suspicious eye. "Sir," he said, "isn't that the man whose laptop caused the breakdown?"

"No," said Graham nervously. "I think it was the goat in the electrical wiring that did it."

"Who are you people? An improv troupe?" Andrew shouted. "Get security up here!"

But it was enough of a distraction for Barney to get into place. Levels below, he and New Ron lay on top of a glass walkway, watching below as Bubble techs sprinted past. They shuffled farther along to the end, where a railing was all that separated them from a giant shaft that led deep under the HQ. A cool wind blew into Barney's face from below, but it was otherwise an endless, sloping void.

"What now?" he asked Marc through his phone.

"Okay, Barney. You're in the right spot," Marc Wydell's voice blared out of the speaker. "You've got to slide down along the central shaft. Then follow it down as far as it goes. Data storage is in the lowest level subbasement."

Barney swung a leg over the rail. The B*Bot climbed over and gripped him tight. And then they jumped. The pair bounded onto a streamlined glass elevator as it rose toward the central data shaft, and then, just as quickly, they clambered from its roof onto the shimmering black cables that led deep into the subterranean core of Bubble.

Sliding down the cables with the weight of New Ron's body on his back, the cold air stung Barney's face worse than any asthma attack he'd ever had. Barney caught a glimpse of something at the bottom.

"Uh, Marc? Did you forget to mention the giant fan?!?" he cried.

"Standby! I'm trying to shut it off!" his remote partner said.

"Standby?!?" Humongous fan blades spun below them, and as the pair slid toward the bottom, the pace became too much. Barney's hand slipped off the bungee-like cable, and the bottom of the shaft grew bigger and bigger in Barney's eyes. So he closed them tight and squeezed his body into a ball as he and New Ron fell into the void.

Clang!!!

Barney looked up and realized the blades had stopped just in time. He landed on the absolute lowest floor of the Bubble Dome with a thud. But his bot had gone blank beside him, its face a plain white screen. No connection here. But it didn't matter now. Barney was about to find the real deal.

CHAPTER 19
SAVED IN THE CLOUD

Floors above, Andrew Morris attempted to bring order to his office and his company. Security and a number of red-eyed B*Bots had Donka and Graham under control. But so long as Barney, New Ron, and Marc remained on the loose, there was still hope.

"Where is your snotty little brat?" the CEO yelled in Graham's face.

"You mean my brave, kind, hero of a kid?!" Dad barked back with an unblinking gaze.

"Mr. Morris, sir!" a tech spoke up. "It appears there's someone inside the Cloud."

"What?!" Andrew said in horror. "It's him, isn't it?"

"He's just looking for his friend," Dad said.

"Friend?!" Andrew laughed while kneeling down to a nearby B*Bot. "Are you my friend, little guy?"

"Sure, Andrew!" the bot replied in a hollow mocking of a chipper tone.

"See? They're just code! A trick!" Andrew said.

"What?"

"Data-harvesting units controlled by us! They're designed to give kids a consumer experience featuring products and services tailored to their browsing profile," the CEO explained.

Graham shook his head in disbelief. "You're spying on these kids."

"So we can sell them stuff! Duh!" Andrew paced manically. "Algorithm for friendship? Uh-uh. Algorithm for profit!"

"Profit from kids?!" Donka asked.

"I HATE KIDS!" Andrew shouted and spun back to his techs. "Now power down the Cloud and send in security!"

But deep in the Cloud, Barney wasted no time running through towering servers as they loomed in endless rows, like an underground city of the future. Their CPUs hummed with low red lights, but between that eerie glow and the total silence, Barney couldn't help but feel that, even though he stood in the center

of the biggest network in the world, this place was
lonely.

"Ron?" he called out in blind hope.
"ROOOOOOOON!"

But nothing called back. There was no signal
from Marc on the phone, so he had to drag the lifeless
B*Bot shell of Ron's former self along as he looked
for a way to connect. Each massive server contained a
foldout keyboard and data ports. Barney walked deep
into the heart of the city, finding the biggest one he
could and logging on using the root passwords Marc
had provided him.

Now how to find Ron? Barney searched for
anything that would lead him to the bot's profile.
"Barney Pudowski . . . Seventh Grade . . . Nonsuch
Middle School . . ." But there was nothing under his
own name. The screen just brought up file after file
of his friends. All the kids had logged back on to their
B*Bots. Their images flooded the screen, streaming
to Barney in real time. Savannah and Rich. Ava and
Noah. They weren't together. They were isolated. They
were all home alone.

At least they had their bots still, Barney thought

as he turned up no sign of Ron.

Of course, things wouldn't be that easy. A
voice suddenly echoed across the cavernous room.
"POWERING DOWN!" it called, and at the far end of
the rows, the red lights began to shut off one by one.
Could Andrew have found him down here? And if so,
would he really shut down the entire Bubble Network
just to stop Barney?

And then, the darkness hit. All around, the electric
lights went out as the network powered down. Barney
stared up at the looming monoliths of data, towering
over him. He shrunk back, the dark, he couldn't . . .

Then, high above, a tiny light shimmered. Barney
stared as it glowed, brighter and brighter. *Ron. The
dark. He knew.*

"Hold on!" he shouted. "I'm coming!"

No more time to worry. Leaving the B*Bot
shell behind, the boy pulled himself up . . . up . . . up
the ladder toward the blinking light that was his last
hope. Arriving at the data port, Barney logged in and
searched with nervous fingers. But he finally found
what he was looking for as a name slowly came to
illuminate the screen.

"Barney? Barney, are you there?" came Marc's voice.

"I'm here! I think I found Ron!"

Barney downloaded the "RONB1NTSATSCO" file, one crazy bit of code within billions of bytes, and then he slid back down to the floor and plugged the tiny drive with the file into Ron's lifeless body. The task bar loaded. 7 percent . . . 12 percent . . . 24 percent. "Come on, Ron!" Barney shouted at the screen, hovering at 88 percent. "I'm here to save you! I *need* you!"

The task bar went blank. Everything was still black. There was no sound. No light. Just the weight of a lifeless B*Bot cradled in Barney's arms. Was it all over?

"Hi, Absalom!" called a cheerful voice as the bot rebooted.

"Ron! It's you!" He embraced the machine that now held the heart of his friend.

"I am within six feet of you!" Ron said.

"You crazy bot!" Barney laughed. "They turned you into electricity and then . . . kind of put you inside a big rock."

Ron looked around the concrete prison. "Electricity is best," he said finally.

In the Cloud, the servers sprung slowly back to half life. A few red lights warming up after the attempted purge of Ron. The B*Bot rolled over to a data port, pulled down his plugs to insert there, and began to hack away at the keys.

"Come on, Ron! We've got to go!" Barney tugged at his arm, but the bot remained firm as he stared at the profiles Barney had pulled up.

"Not not your friends. They are not having fun," he said. Barney checked back to the monitor, and his search for the kids from Nonsuch had strangely revealed a side of them that Barney had never seen before.

There was Savannah, curled in a ball on her bed while hundreds of "Poop Girl" pop-ups spun all around her. Rich stood on the seesaw at the park, trying to launch himself into the air, but the video counter read "0 views." Noah mashed buttons away on a game controller in his room, but his bot projected a huge top ten score list where "Noah" was the only name. And Ava ran around her room with a pained smile, desperately arranging clothes and shoes to be half in shot as if she was surrounded by people.

"They look so lonely," Barney said. "I used to think I was the lonely one, but they need a friend more than I do. They need to upgrade to a Ron."

"I am *for* making friends," Ron said with a ping.

"Wait . . . you mean it? You can upgrade their bots so they're more like you?" Barney laughed. "Two hundred and twenty-five million Rons out there. It'd be insane! I mean, amazing but . . ."

"It will be fun," Ron said. "Just please connect me to the Bubble Network."

"We're right here in the middle of it now," Barney marveled. "This may be our one chance."

He brought down a cable from the terminal and began to connect it to Ron, giving a play-by-play to Marc as he went. When the connection came online, Barney smiled and said, "Hang on, guys! You're getting a Ron!"

But as the transfer started, Ron's face began to glitch *hard.* And moment by moment, the light drained from the B*Bot.

"No, no . . . Ron, where are you going?!"

"The Bubble Network. I will stay here and learn stuff about friends."

"Can't you just . . . copy yourself and send that?!?"

"The settings have not been uploaded," Ron replied.

Marc's voice called on Barney's phone. "His code is fragmenting. He can't come back from this."

"No! You're coming with me!" Barney cried and clung to the little bot's body.

"I will make five hundred million friends. I am *for* making friends, Barney," Ron said. "Just like you taught me."

"No. *Stay with me*, remember?" The tears were welling in Barney's eyes.

Ron projected a memory of their friendship vision board, but "Stay With Me" had been crossed out and replaced.

"Stay friends?" Ron said. And Barney knew that this had to be a two-way street.

"I guess . . . we'll swap all of the B*Bots for a real friend now, huh? The best one."

"You will have friends to sit with at recess," Ron promised.

"Okay," Barney said. "Go, Ron. You don't have to stay within six feet. Be everywhere!"

"Au revoir, Absalom," the B*Bot said.

"Arrivederci, Ron Binscatsco!" Barney replied.

And with one last keystroke, Ron's body went dark. The room around them, though, burned bright red with energy as a formula more complicated than anything ever programmed in a lab shot through the circuits of the Bubble Network at lightspeed. The code's takeover was instantaneous in Marc's lab, and as soon as he saw it, the Bubble founder knew how much Ron—and Barney—had given up to help him achieve his vision.

"It's not an upgrade unless it affects the whole system," Marc said to himself as the beauty of Ron's mutating code filled his screen. He quickly hooked up the data to the entire Bubble Network. "Upgrade all B*Bots to RONB1NTSATSCO's settings. Of course! His code is the fix to mine!"

With Barney's final push on the Enter key, the B*Bots changed forever. Though, as the lights came back up all over the Bubble Dome, almost no one was aware of how much things were about to change. Only

Barney and his family, even despite being escorted out of the building by security, could really feel the excitement of what was coming.

Back in the Bubble Dome's launchitorium, the smoke had cleared and the lasers powered down on the stage, but the assembled employees of Bubble were still milling around waiting for the updated plans of Andrew Morris. The CEO took the stage in a rush, absent-mindedly saying into the mic, "Sorry . . . just . . . um. Where were we?"

Andrew swiped through some slides from his presentation, but with a sudden flicker, the screens behind him morphed into something else altogether. It was video footage of Andrew himself, shouting wildly in the Bubble lab earlier that day.

". . . A trick! Data-harvesting units controlled by us . . . so we can sell them stuff!" he shouted as the image fast-forwarded in a blur to a close-up of his face screaming, "I HATE KIDS!"

The crowd erupted in gasps and boos as Andrew's face lost all its color. But the mood turned as the employees parted to make way for Marc Wydell, who casually strolled up with this hand on the phone that had recorded Andrew's meltdown.

Defeated, Andrew slunk back and mumbled into the microphone, "You know, I've loved my time as Bubble's CEO. And I want to thank you all for your support over the last thirty-two historic hours. But I need to go now to spend more time with my . . . contacts. So please, welcome back Marc Wydell."

Andrew retreated backstage, fighting off embarrassed tears while Marc ascended the stage to cheers. He had the real algorithm now, one that had the essence of real friendship: unpredictability. "Welcome," he said, "to the future of friendship!"

CHAPTER 20
CORD CUTTERS

Even three months after the infiltration of Bubble Corporation, the world still hadn't gone back to normal. Except in one respect: Barney still didn't have a Bubble Bot.

He still saw them everywhere in Nonsuch, of course. But watching other kids play with B*Bots didn't feel too different from watching other kids play with anyone. As his class broke for recess, Barney stepped onto the playground and watched as a boy with a bot skinned like a troll tried and failed to command his companion to play his way.

"Here we go again," the kid said to the distracted B*Bot. "What happened to staying within six feet of me?"

"I get to choose!" said the trollbot, suddenly

151

reskinning itself in disco lights and dancing wildly to the latest K-pop song craze.

"K-pop, are you kidding me?" The kid laughed. "Three months it's been like this! Are they *ever* gonna fix you?"

"Are they ever gonna fix *you*?" the dancing bot replied with a mischievous smile before speeding off across the playground and instigating a new game of tag.

"Hey," came a voice from behind Barney. He turned to find Savannah Meades, casually leaning on a seat. "You changed the world, Barney Pudowski. How cool is that?"

"It wasn't just me who did it." Barney smiled, seeing Ron in every rogue friendship bot that spun by. The bots no longer spat out predetermined personalities or divided kids into camps. Their tech wasn't just to rack up points in some invisible game. Instead, the B*Bots listened to kids. And disagreed with them sometimes. And always, always stuck by their sides. Even if no one really knew what had happened, they all knew the bots were different now—they were better somehow.

"Oh my gosh!" called a girl new to the middle school, running up to Savannah like she just saw a celebrity. "Aren't you that girl who got . . . you know . . . ?"

The girl's bot made a scan of Savannah's, but within seconds it made a negative chirp and replied, "Savannah Meades has only five friends. No videos found."

"Oh . . . my bad," the girl said with a blush and walked off.

Savannah smiled a real, genuine smile and punched Barney softly on the shoulder. "Thanks for that, too," she said.

"Come on," Barney replied and led them across the yard. As they walked, every stray bot spun over to give Barney a quick high five as the other kids whispered, "There goes Pudowski . . . my bot does that every time to him . . . He's like the king of bots and he doesn't even have one!"

They made their way over to the spot formerly known as the Friendstop — a fixture of the playground now proudly labeled "The Barney Bench," where Noah, Ava, and Rich waited as always.

"Barn, man, you have to get back into that Bubble Cloud place," Noah said as he patted his own gamer bot on its side. "Just long enough to get this bot to stop making up its own game rules."

"Free armor upgrade for everyone!" the bot chirped as its internal processors doled out items for all of Noah's potential competitors.

"How am I ever gonna get the high score now?" the boy groaned.

"Shhhhhh!" Rich silenced talk of the Bubble Cloud mission as he turned to Barney in a hushed tone. "Dude! We gotta tell 'em! You pranked a global freakin' tech giant, man! Please let me stream the reveal, bro . . . please!"

"Sorry, Rich, but the best I can offer you guys is one of these," said Barney, opening up his lunch box and revealing a fresh batch of Donka's chicken feet. They mock toasted each other with the food and then dug in.

"Is all your gran's food this good?" Rich asked.

"Come over sometime to hang and find out," Barney said. "I know you're all dying to see my rock collection." And they all laughed, but they agreed.

"So long as you talk to that goat, because I do not want any more of my jewelry going through his lower intestine." Savannah smiled.

It felt good to be here with his oldest friends. And when their B*Bots came rolling alongside, he felt a little thrill of recognition from each one's smile. Each was a little bit goofy, a little bit glitchy, a little bit Ron.